A Bigfoot's Gift

Mel Braxton

for Kimber
May you find strength
even when it's hard
to fit in.
♦ Mel Braxton

for the misfits

Chapter 1

"Come on, Alice, let's play!" Bryson said while we waited in a forest clearing.

"Playing is for children," I said, turning to look at the five-year-old I was currently responsible for. "Besides, we promised Pa we'd stay here."

"Do you really want to sit around waiting for Ma and Pa?" he asked.

"No," I replied, but Bryson already knew that. I'd been complaining for weeks about today. I hadn't daydreamed about my suitor when I was younger and wasn't going to start now.

"Then let's play a game." Bryson begged with his big brown eyes. I couldn't say no when he looked at me like that, and he knew it. "It's Solstice morning. Why do we have to sit around and wait for the adults? Let's do something!"

My fingers pulled at my fur. It'd been thoroughly brushed by Stepma that morning. I felt like a soft teddy bear, not a Bigfoot, but Stepma had insisted.

"Okay, fine," I said. "What game are we playing?"

"Hide and seek!" Bryson jumped with excitement. "I'll count, and you hide?

"Sure."

"Our only rule is don't cross the boundary!" he said.

"Course I'm not going to cross the boundary!" I'd be in trouble for leaving the clearing, but Pa would skin me alive if he caught me crossing the boundary.

Bryson leaned his head against a tree and shielded his eyes. He began counting.

I ran away, my bare, hairy feet were silent against the forest floor. Pa had shown me how to run quietly when I was a child, and the skill had come as natural to me as it did any young Bigfoot.

I reached the hilltop and began to climb my favorite pine tree. Bryson would know to look for me here, but that didn't matter. This was where I wanted to be.

My fur caught in the branches while I pulled myself up. Stepma would be furious with me, but there was a good view higher up. It'd be worth it.

I kept going, ignoring the tree creaking beneath me. I was getting bigger and needed to stop climbing the old tree. But not today.

The only memories I had of my real Ma were from the base of this tree, but that wasn't the only reason it was my favorite.

It was the best tree because of the view.

I reached the top and looked around. Not only was this tree on the hilltop, but it was at the edge of the boundary. By looking behind me, I could see the Bigfoot village and the farmland that surrounded it.

If I looked forward, I could see beyond, where the humans lived.

A path called a highway twisted and turned like a river. Bug-like objects called cars shuffled along its length. Another village was tucked into the valley. It was where the humans lived.

I squinted and allowed the boundary to catch in the light. Its golden reflection glinted in reply.

Don't cross the boundary. It was the first rule Pa ever taught me. It was the first lesson every child learned.

The boundary was the barrier separating my people from humans. We're Bigfoot. We have big feet, tall figures, and brown hair that covers our entire bodies. Ma told me the humans call us Bigfoot, Sasquatch, and other names too. They pretend there is only one of us, not an entire tribe.

We're hidden so well that humans think we're myths. Pa says our lives depend on keeping that myth alive. Grandma had said that before him and her grandpa had said it before her. The humans would hunt us if they knew we were real— destroying our people as if we were less than them.

As the legends have it, when the humans began to claim our lands, our people prayed to the Fae for protection. The Fae work in subtle ways, but this time, they gave my people a clear message. The Fae gave the Bigfoot people a gift: The Crux. Its enchantment protected those within its boundaries from the awareness of humans.

My ear twitched. There was a snap of branches below me and the rustle of leaves. The hair along my spine rose.

I scanned the ground but couldn't find the source of the noise. The sounds continued. They were too crude to be an animal, and no Bigfoot walked that loudly.

Human, perhaps.

I took a long inhale, studying the scent. Artificial fragrances disguised anything earthy about this creature.

Definitely smelled like a human.

I leapt from my tree, landing soundlessly on my feet, and shifted my gaze to check that the boundary remained a few feet away. Whoever was on the opposite side wouldn't be able to see me.

It was easy to see the human through the brush. Its clothes were camouflaged, but the movement gave them away.

It was rare to see a human this close to the boundary. Usually, the Fae magic guided them away from our valley. Unless, of course, the Fae wanted a human to get close, that was in their power too.

I waited and was rewarded when the human came closer. It looked to be male. He was maybe a hand or two shorter than me, an adolescent perhaps. His face seemed youthful too. He could be the same age as me. What was it like to be a human my age, would he be anything like me?

Could he understand how it felt to be between childhood and adolescence? Would he know how being fourteen-years-old was like being in the cross-section between childhood and adulthood?

I didn't enjoy Bryson and his games anymore, but I wasn't ready to have a mate either. Maybe that was the real reason I'd said yes to Bryson's game. I didn't like waiting around the clearing for Pa to bring a suitor to me.

If only I were a better daughter. Then I would've helped Pa find my mate and become a model female in the village. Maybe I wasn't a good daughter.

More likely, the human wouldn't understand any of that. He was probably too different from me to relate.

The human's face was hairless and pink as raw skin. It made me squeamish just looking at it—humans were so exposed.

I had no idea what he could possibly be tracking, but he continued to walk towards me. The boundary ensured that he was completely unaware that a Bigfoot was now only a few feet away.

I studied his clumsy movement. He wore clunky boots over his feet. I dug my toes into the earth below and considered how vulnerable human feet were. I celebrated how secure I felt with my oversized, hairy feet. I was built to be wild and couldn't imagine living with his weakness.

The boy held a bow, but it was nothing like the ones used in the village. It wasn't sleek but had rough angles. It wasn't made of wood. He held the weapon awkwardly. Clearly, he had no idea what he was doing.

He moved towards the boundary. For a moment I was afraid that he'd pass right through, but he stopped short of the line.

I'd never been this close to a human before and studied the boy with intrigue. A few strands of dark hair escaped from his hat. I caught a glimpse of his eyes, they were startlingly light, and I looked away. His clothes appeared too big for him, like they were meant for someone else.

"Serves me right," he said to himself, "course I couldn't prove him wrong. I really am terrible at this."

He set the bow aside and sat on the ground. He looked over the same view I'd been admiring.

He seemed sad. If he had been my friend, I would've asked what was wrong. Maybe there was a way I could help.

But he wasn't my friend. He was human, and I was Bigfoot. But…I could see our similarities. We looked different, but I didn't imagine his sadness and desperation. His emotions were as real and tangible as my own.

I considered the bow next to him. This boy wasn't dangerous.

Maybe I could meet him. I had so many questions to ask. What was it like to be human?

I raised my hand and reached forward. I'd tap his shoulder. I located the boundary again and, holding my breath, let my fingers slip through to the other side—

"Alice!" Pa shouted. I pulled my hand back.

The boy must have sensed something. He sprang to his feet and drew the bow.

I hadn't heard Pa arrive, but I turned to see his face scrunched in rage. I felt the presence of his height, his strength. I was definitely in trouble.

Bryson was at Pa's feet, his face apologetic.

"Don't you dare cross that boundary!" Pa grabbed my wrist and pulled me back.

"Ouch! You're hurting me!" I squirmed from him.

Pa dropped my arm. He'd never really hurt me, but he sure was scary. He took a long breath and lowered himself so we could meet face-to-face.

"What were you planning to do?" he asked.

"The boy seemed lonely," I replied.

"He has a bow."

"He doesn't know how to use it!" I pointed to the boy, still searching for the source of the noise. His posture was rigid and useless. "Look at him."

"They're killers. How can you, of all people, forget that?"

He was referring to Ma. I hated it when he brought her up. He told me she had been taken captive by the humans, but I remember the day she left. She had crossed the boundary by her own free will.

When she didn't return, she was presumed dead. I even attended her funeral. It was the reason I had a step-ma and a half-brother.

I loved hearing about her, but Pa never spoke of Ma unless it was to discipline me. He never answered my questions about who she'd been and why she'd crossed the boundary.

"We should go," Pa said. "Your suitor is waiting for you."

I looked at my fur and considered cleaning it but thought better of it. Whoever my suitor was, he might as well know the type of female that I was.

Chapter 2

Pa led me back to the clearing where the others were waiting for us.

Stepma ran to me, shielding the other Bigfoots from my view. Her face was bright with criticism, so I held her gaze until she looked away. She patted my fur and frowned. "It'll have to do," she said.

Despite our different blood, Stepma was a true mother to me. She had cared for me after my ma had disappeared, even before she and Pa were a mated pair.

She reached for my hand, and I let her hold it. "Come along," she said.

Stepma led me into the clearing to meet my suitor, the one that she and Pa had selected for me. This suitor wouldn't necessarily become my mate, but I was expected to court him until the Winter Solstice.

If, by winter, we wanted to become a mated pair, then we would be joined at the Winter Ceremony. We would be given a small house in the village and encouraged to start a family of our own.

If we decided to part ways, our parents would choose another suitor for us, and the process would start over. This ritual started now that I was fourteen and would repeat until my eighteenth summer. If I didn't pick a mate by then, I'd move to the dorms with the other single adults. Sometimes mates found each other there, but others preferred to be alone.

I figured I was the type to be alone. But first, I had to wait through four years of courtships.

I once asked Stepma about her courtships. Usually, she'd answer all my questions, but when it came to courtship, she had shrugged her shoulders and said, "It's tradition. But don't worry, we've a great suitor in mind."

I had nodded. Even if I didn't want a mate, I did trust my parents to choose a good suitor.

Stepma stepped aside, and I saw the three Bigfoots standing on the opposite side of the clearing. I knew him immediately.

"Daylen," I said as Stepma pulled me to the center of the clearing. I'd known him since childhood. However, since he lived on the opposite side of the village, we hadn't seen each other often.

He was a year or two older than me. I wouldn't be his first suitor. That was fine with me, maybe he might understand this relationship better than I did.

The last time I'd seen him, his limbs were too long, and his movements were awkward. Now he was starting to become an adult. His muscles had grown toned, and his childhood grace had transformed into powerful strength.

Several long gashes glinted red on his forearm. A fresh wound that looked like a bear attack. It would scar. It told me he was part of the hunting party. That didn't surprise me, Pa was a leader among the hunters and would've favored one for my suitor.

"Alice," Daylen said. His voice had changed too, it had a lower tone now.

Despite myself, my stomach fluttered. My heart began to pound. My brain grew fuzzy.

Now that I was before him, I cared about the dirt in my fur, the way my hair lay less than perfect. I hoped Daylen would still find me attractive. Despite all my reservations, I wanted him to find me desirable—

I blushed at the thought and stepped back towards my family. Bryson offered to take my hand, but I shook my head, that'd be childish.

I glared at Pa. Like Stepma had promised, they'd done well with this first choice. Pa stood straighter and chuckled. Then he laughed, his deep rumble filling the clearing.

Stepma followed suit, and soon Daylen's family was laughing too. Daylen didn't laugh. It was a joke I refused to understand. Nothing was funny about what was happening here.

I found what remained of my pride and nodded towards Pa. I'd accept his choice in suitor.

"Does anyone object?" Pa asked.

Nobody did.

"Excellent," Daylen's pa said.

I waited, but nothing else happened. That was it, no real ceremony. We met, and nobody said no. Daylen and I were suitors.

Daylen stepped forward and met my eyes. They were a lighter brown than most, almost green in places. The effect gave him a brightness that was unique among Bigfoots.

To my own surprise, I began to look forward to being Daylen's suitor.

The excitement must have shown on my face because Pa laughed again. "Well, get on with it," he said. "Enjoy the holiday. We'll see you at the celebration tonight."

Daylen reached forward and touched my hand. I pulled away—not because I minded his touch—but because it was electrifying.

"I was thinking we'd go trapping today," he said. "I know it's not traditional, but your pa recommended I set up some snares last night. Want to see if I caught anything?"

I was worried we would have to spend the day as other foolish young suitors might: wandering through the flower fields or laying on a hill admiring cloud patterns. Trapping was at least practical. The game was smaller than that brought in during the big hunts but still necessary to village life.

"Where did you set up the snares?" I asked.

"Northridge," he replied.

"Then let's go." I turned towards the main path. It was time to get away from our parents.

"See you tonight," he said to our families before jogging towards the main trail.

I kissed Bryson on the head and ran after Daylen.

We ran to the main trail that ran between the farms and the forested land.

The trail widened. I caught up to Daylen and fell into stride next to him.

"Snares," I said. "Good thinking."

"Your pa said you'd like it."

"It's not a feminine trade—" I began, but stopped. I didn't want to embarrass myself.

He didn't say anything.

"How did you get that?" I asked. "The slash on your arm."

He put his hand to the bright red wound. "Hunting," he said.

"Recently?"

"Two days ago."

"I hope it heals well," I said.

He didn't reply. Silence again.

"How is your sister? Maime, right?" I asked.

"She is good. Took her suitor last winter. Now she is pregnant."

"Your parents must be thrilled."

"They are," he agreed.

I waited for him to say something more, or maybe ask me a question. He didn't.

"How was your last suitor?" I asked.

He switched to a walk, turning to look my way. "Do you always ask this many questions?"

I slowed, matching his speed. "I like to think curiosity is one of my best attributes."

He laughed. "Do you know what humans say about curiosity?"

"No," I said.

"It's what killed the cat."

"What does that mean?" I asked.

"Nothing, really."

"You're not making any sense."

"Maybe that's my point," he said. "Not everything makes sense. You can't know everything."

"That doesn't stop me from trying!"

He began to run again. "Come on, if we're going to bring any game back in time for the celebration, we should keep going."

I started running too. "What about—"

"It's my turn to ask questions," Daylen interrupted. "What trade are you studying?"

That was one question I had been hoping to avoid. I had wondered if my lack of trade had made it difficult for Pa to find me a suitor. By my age, I should've picked a trade and begun contributing to the village

"I suppose I do a little bit of everything," I finally said.

"You haven't picked a trade yet?" He seemed surprised, I should have expected this. "You're not even down to a couple?"

"I'm not lazy!" I protested. "I do all sorts of things. I help Stepma around the house, and when she doesn't need me, I ask around to see if anyone else needs a hand. I know all sorts of useful things."

"What kinds of things?" he asked.

"I can weave and prepare herbs. I help shear the sheep then make yarn. Sometimes I care for the hens. I help with the farms. I've even repaired a house."

"Do you have a favorite trade?" he asked.

"I don't like taking care of the children."

"But you're good with Bryson. I've seen you two together."

"He's my baby brother," I replied. "Course I'm good with him."

Daylen nodded.

"That's a lie," I said. "I do have a favorite trade."

"You do?" he asked.

"I wanted to become a hunter when I was little."

He laughed. "That's male work."

It had been a joke, and I laughed with him. "I know. Maybe that's why I wanted it."

"Well, I won't show you how to hunt," he said, "but I'll show you how to trap."

He began to run again, and I fell into pace beside him.

My heart raced with more than the exercise. Despite all my anticipation, Solstice day was going much better than I had ever expected.

Chapter 3

Daylen's traps proved he was a good hunter. The snares were filled, the kills were clean. I studied his work as he reset the traps, listening carefully as he answered my questions. Regardless of what happened between us, I decided that I'd learn to trap because of him.

We found a flow to our work. Walk, check the trap, empty it, reset, and move forward. We only paused long enough for a small lunch that Daylen had packed: nuts, berries, jerky, and cheese.

Soon, I discovered I was actually enjoying my time with him. Usually, silence bothered me, but sharing it with Daylen felt natural. I began imagining a future with him and discovered the idea appealed to me. That realization made me feel sick. I had never wanted to have a mate, but now I was swooning over my first suitor.

We reached the final trap when the sun was high in the sky. After we were done resetting it, Daylen carried a heavy sack back to the village.

We took the game to the cookhouse and spread out the animals on a back table. Together, we began skinning and gutting our catch. It was mostly rabbits and squirrels, but we had caught one raccoon and a fox.

Working with the dead animals was more male work. However, Pa had shown it to me before, and Daylen wasn't afraid to teach me anything I couldn't remember. Knowing Daylen didn't care how I fit into our traditional roles helped me build the confidence to be myself with him.

The cooks took the meat, grumbling that it had arrived so late in the day. We ignored them and took the half-cleaned skins to the tannery so they could be cured.

By the time we were done, the sun hung low in the sky. My stomach whined. Today was the longest day of the year and, somehow, I'd been busy for all of it. I stretched, bathing in the sunlight, miraculously comfortable with my new suitor.

I evaluated myself and, with horror, discovered that not only was my fur matted, but I smelled like animal guts. I could not go to my first Solstice Celebration as an adolescent smelling like animal!

I pulled my arms to my side, trying to cover the smell. I glanced at Daylen, but he didn't seem to notice. If I left now, there would be enough time to groom before the bonfire.

"I'll see you tonight," I said, already walking towards home.

"You're leaving?" he asked.

"Yeah," —I couldn't tell him I smelled bad!— "I want to go check on Bryson." That made no sense, Bryson would be playing with the other children, but Daylen might not know that.

I left Daylen behind and began running as soon as I was out of his sight.

Stepma was home but didn't ask any questions when I grabbed my towel, soap, and brush. I ran from the house and to the river.

There was a spot on the river where the water barely flowed. It was a common bathing area but was deserted this late in the day. I was running late. It'd take a miracle for my fur to dry in time, but at least I wouldn't smell.

Using the soap, I scrubbed my fur harder than ever. I cursed every imperfection in my body—the way my hair was always straight when it should curl or curly when it should lay flat. The wet hair clung to my body, showing my shape and reminding me how disproportionated I had become. I'd grown tall and lanky, but my body was still shaped like a child.

Daylen could never be attracted to someone like me, but I had to try.

I detangled my fur, drying it as I went. I was halfway done when I glanced at the sun. It was hovering on the horizon. Soon, it'd disappear, and then the Solstice Ceremony would begin.

I sped through the remaining work and, unsatisfied, tucked the supplies under a nearby tree. I began running towards the village.

I watched the sun setting behind the hill and, squinting my eyes, confirmed that it hovered above the hilltop.

There was enough time, but I had to hurry. Once the sun vanished, I'd be late. I ran to the campfire hill.

I passed a lit torch in the hands of Mother Gazina. That was a good sign. The Ceremony wouldn't begin until she started it. She was standing with an apprentice and four couples. These were the suitors who would become mates during the Solstice Ceremony.

Mother Gazina's voice followed me as I ran past them. "Careful, child."

I ran faster. I could hear the chorus now, the Song of Summer. My people sang thanks to the sun for the gift of daylight. We celebrated the long days and the time for growth that the summer gave. The final verse would thank the Fae for their protection.

I reached the fire pit as the song's second verse began. I jumped to the nearest log and, using its height, scanned the far side of the fire pit. That was where the other adolescents sat and where I belonged now that I had a suitor.

I was embarrassed to be running late. I could finally sit with the adolescents and annoyed that I was making a scene.

I found Daylen, sitting a few rows back. It looked like there was space near him. He was waiting for me.

I jumped from the log and ran towards him. He saw me and smiled. He seemed happy to see me!

My heart jumped into my throat, and my legs wobbled.

I leapt towards the open space, landing with a wet foot against a smooth stone.

Normally, I was graceful. I should've been able to catch myself. But with Daylen's eyes on me, my body failed.

My foot slipped.

I fell, my butt smacking against the ground in front of the entire village.

I sprang to my feet, and brought my hands to my backside, trying to wipe it clean. My wet fur had picked up dirt during the fall, transforming it into slick mud that now covered my backside. My attempts to clean it only smeared it.

Someone sitting with the adolescents laughed. Others joined them. There were attempts to hush the sound, but I heard it anyhow.

My ears grew hot. I held my eyes open and bit my lip, willing myself not to cry.

I dared to look at Daylen. He was smiling like the whole thing had been a clever joke. Then he motioned for me to join him.

The song continued uninterrupted. It was now the third and final verse. Mother Gazina was at the crowd's perimeter, holding her torch high, and walking towards the fire pit.

I swallowed and took a moment to catch my breath.

But I lost it again the second I saw who was standing behind Mother Gazina.

Jaria.

Like Mother Gazina, Jaria wore a long robe and a hood that shadowed her face. I hadn't recognized her when I'd run by earlier.

But now that I had time to study her, there was no denying it. The female behind Mother Gazina was Jaria.

Jaria.

She'd been my best friend when we were children, but had vanished two years ago. Her parents swore she'd return and never held a funeral. Regardless, I'd grieved for her.

But her parents had been right. Jaria had returned. Now she was apprenticed to the Mother herself.

I stared at my oldest friend, forgetting my embarrassing fall and the mud across my back. None of that mattered anymore. Jaria was alive!

Chapter 4

Mother Gazina lit the bonfire, and the licking flames devoured the ready branches.

I tried to study Jaria, convincing myself she was real, but she was blocked from view by the couple standing closest to me. I'd played with both of them as children but never would've guessed they'd become mates. Regardless, their smiles were radiant.

But it was even stranger to see Jaria alive. If she was back, why hadn't she come to find me? I thought we'd been close friends. She and I had sworn to avoid suitors when we were children. Didn't that bond us for life?

Jaria was a little older than me and had begun exploring trades before me. In retrospect, I wondered if that was when she began studying with Mother Gazina, but that didn't explain where Jaria had been during the last two years.

The Ceremony continued, oblivious to my questions.

As Mother Gazina introduced the couples, I shifted towards Daylen as they said their vows. I wondered what would happen to us over the next six months. Would we be speaking our own promises at the Winter Solstice?

As Mother Gazina led the couples through the words, everyone played their part as citizens of the village. We swore that we had witnessed their promises and would do all in our power to strengthen these new families.

After the joining, we paid tribute to those who had died since the Winter Solstice. Mother Gazina spoke their names, and we echoed them after her. Seven of the deceased had been elders, their passing had been tranquil, and we said their names with ease.

However, when Mother Gazina came to the last two names, the village struggled to repeat after her. The names belonged to a mother and her babe. She had died during childbirth, and the child had been lost the following day. It was a tragedy, unusual but not unique.

After a pause, Mother Gazina reached the third part of The Solstice Ceremony. She asked the families of the babies born since Winter Solstice to come forward.

The mood lightened as numerous families stepped toward the fire. Ten infants had been born since the last Solstice, and their families shuffled to crowd around the fire pit.

I recalled the Solstice after Bryson had been born. I had presented him with my family, and Stepma had let me carry him. That was the day I promised myself I'd do all I could to help her with Bryson. Hearing the newly made vows for the infants always reminded me of that oath. Even though I was now an adolescent, Bryson still needed his big sister.

Mother Gazina honored each of the infants in turn. The community spoke our own commitment to raising them as part of our people.

Mother Gazina dismissed the families and circled the bonfire. Despite her age, she was formidable. Her strength wasn't in power but presence. She radiated authority. Mother Gazina faced the fire and held her torch high. She began the Solstice prayer.

"We thank the earth that provides, the water that nourishes, the fire that fuels, and the air that binds everything together. We thank the Spirit for all that we share and all that we are. The Fae have provided for us. Let us celebrate on this, the shortest of nights!"

She finished the prayer by throwing her torch into the burning fire.

I was supposed to look away at this point in the Ceremony, everyone was. Pa himself had covered my eyes as a child so that I wouldn't peek. This fire was sacred.

But I wasn't standing with Pa anymore. While my peers ducked their heads, I looked forward, directly into the flame.

It wasn't that I was brave, it was that I didn't have a choice.

Some force had taken over my body, rejecting my efforts to lower my neck and close my eyes.

When the torch made contact, I watched as the fire grew higher. The heat from it was familiar, but not the sight. The flickering flames began changing colors, transforming with hues of green, blue, and purple.

My eyes widened with awe.

At first, there'd been no pattern, but then the colors mixed together. An image appeared, ghostly within the flames.

A face. I shouldn't have been able to recognize her—it'd been too many years—but I knew who she was.

Ma, my real ma, looked at me from within the flames.

I shifted within the crowd and walked forward. Others parted around me, controlled by the same force that pulled me to the fire.

My ma reached her hand towards me. She motioned for me to get closer.

I extended my own hand, transfixed by the thought of touching my mother again…

Before I realized what I'd done, my hand was in the fire.

I prepared to scream, expecting burning pain. But this didn't hurt. Tickled, perhaps, but my hand was only as warm as Ma's embrace had been.

I looked to the flame, searching for Ma, but the image had vanished.

Panicked, I tried to pull my hand from the fire, but the hold on my body remained.

Then I felt the touch of someone's hand on my shoulder. Gentle but strong.

"I'm with you," Mother Gazina said. I wasn't sure I should trust her, but foreign energy was building within me. I was like a dam about to break. I stopped resisting and opened myself to the force pushing into me.

My mind went blank.

Then I felt them, the Fae, as they probed my mind, exploring my being, working to understand who I was. They evaluated every element of me.

I heard their giggles as slowly, one layer at a time, they peeled me open until I didn't feel like I was Alice anymore.

The laughter continued.

My head stung, like pinpricks against my skull. I tried to ignore the sensation, but it felt wrong, invasive.

I pulled back.

Someone grabbed my other shoulder, keeping me in place. They held me stable as the Fae wandered my mind.

I didn't know how much time passed, it may have been moments or the entire night.

Then—with one final shrill of laughter—the moment passed.

The bonfire was orange again, and my hand hung over its kissing flames. My fur was healthy and unburned.

I blinked my eyes, clearing my vision, and looked away from the flame.

As I stepped back, I realized I was holding something inside my palm. I opened my hand and found I was holding a transparent crystal. A hole had been cut through the base, and a leather strap had been pushed through, turning the stone into a pendant. It was a gem that could be worn.

My stomach clenched. I'd seen something like this before.

My ma had worn a crystal like this, I could remember it. It was a memento I had wanted, but it disappeared with her.

I turned away from the fire and looked up to see Jaria standing in front of me. Just as she had done at this moment, she was the one who had steadied me when I'd struggled.

Our gaze locked. There was something, part admiration and part pity, in her perspective that I couldn't quite understand.

I stepped away but knew this wasn't something I could run from.

I looked down, and my heart leapt as I realized Jaria was wearing a quartz stone of her own. It was attached to a leather strap and wrapped around her wrist. That was the same way Ma had worn her own crystal.

"Welcome," she said, acknowledging me for the first time that evening.

I glanced back at her face and heard a roar of applause. The Ceremony was over. The Solstice Celebration was about to begin.

Chapter 5

The Solstice Celebration was an excuse for excess. Music would play half the night, food was prepared in large quantities, and some would even stay awake through the night to welcome the dawn.

Even with a suitor, I'd been looking forward to tonight. It was my first Solstice as an adolescent, and I was finally free to stay as late as I wanted.

But now, as I stared at Jaria, my excitement evaporated.

Jaria had changed. She wasn't the girl who had vanished two years ago. There was a depth to her eyes that I didn't recognize.

I reached out to hug her.

She pulled away.

"Where have you been?" I asked.

"It doesn't matter, I'm back now," she replied.

I glanced towards Mother Gazina. "You're apprenticed to the Mother, aren't you?"

"I am."

I studied her, stunned and unsure how to respond. I was thrilled to see her, but she didn't seem ready to see me. Jaria had always been complicated, but now there was a darkness to her that hadn't been there before.

"What happened to you?" I asked.

She ignored my question and asked her own, "What did you see when you looked into the fire?"

"I saw my ma," I said, realizing Jaria could be a source of answers. "Was my ma really here? Is she alive?"

"That wasn't your ma," Jaria said. "Just a Fae trick."

"Are you sure? It really looked like her!" I didn't know how badly I needed that image to have been real until Jaria said it wasn't.

Jaria rolled her eyes in response. It was like she was saying there was no reason to fight over this, I wouldn't understand.

Then she grabbed my hand, the one holding the crystal pendant. She yanked my hand upward, pulling the crystal towards her face.

"You'll want to keep that close," she said, studying it. "It's up to you to learn what it can do."

She plucked the crystal from my hand and tied a few knots in the cord. She lifted it upward and dropped it over my head. My chest warmed as the stone made contact with my fur.

Jaria seemed disappointed when nothing happened.

"Do you know what it is?" I asked, pointing to the stone wrapped around her own wrist. "Where did you get yours? My ma had one too, did she get it from the fire?"

"So many questions, Alice." It was the first time I'd heard her say my name. I didn't feel welcomed, only tolerated.

She turned towards Mother Gazina.

I reached for her hand. "Jaria, I've—I missed you."

She didn't turn back.

"I thought you were dead…I grieved for you," I continued.

"Nobody said I was dead." She pulled her hand from my grasp.

"What happened to you?" This wasn't the Jaria I remembered.

She didn't reply but didn't move away. I waited, stilling my urge to ask more questions.

Finally, she faced me and said, "Alice, it wasn't my choice to leave. I'm sorry if that hurt you, but I can't be your friend. It might be hard to understand, but I'm not who I used to be."

She moved away. I watched her go and join Mother Gazina. They retreated in silence towards the Mother's house.

I wanted to yell, to thrash, anything to express my sudden grief, rage, and confusion. I'd already lost Jaria once. I'd lost my ma as well. Seeing both of them tore my grief wide open, allowing the pain to seep back into my life.

I didn't know how to express myself, and so I stood, stunned, as they entered their house.

Someone touched my shoulder. I turned to see Daylen beside me. "Who was that?" he asked.

"Do you remember Jaria?" I said.

He nodded. "Strange girl. I thought she died."

"That was her. We were close, once."

He nodded again, there wasn't anything else to say.

"That's pretty," he said, pointing to the pendant. "Did she give that to you?"

I considered the crystal and realized that Daylen hadn't seen—that nobody had seen—me reach into the fire. I thought of telling Daylen what had happened, but now that the moment had passed, it seemed too strange. The pendant was the only evidence I had that any of it had been real.

"Yes, Jaria gave it to me," I finally chose to say.

"Well then," he said, handing me a cup of sweet drink. "Now that you're a proper adolescent, you should enjoy the festivity."

The drink was refreshing, I had been so busy all day that I had forgotten to enjoy myself.

Another male stepped forward. I recognized him, but his name escaped me.

"I'm Heron," he said. "And who are you? Hardly matters!" He slapped my back, forcing my drink to spill out of the cup. "You're Daylen's suitor!"

"This is Alice," Daylen said for me.

"Nice fall," Heron said.

I blushed. Between the Fae, Jaria, and the pendant, I'd actually forgotten my embarrassing entrance.

"But understandable. After all, Daylen is your suitor. It's only natural to fall at his feet." To make his point, Heron comedically fell to the ground and jumped back to his feet.

Daylen laughed. The mockery made me angry, but Daylen didn't see that.

"We went trapping today," Daylen said. "Alice can take care of herself. You know who her father is, don't you?"

"Your father?" Heron asked, evaluating me from top to bottom. "You're Caiman's girl? Daughter of his first mate—the one that disappeared?"

I nodded, shocked that someone would mention Ma so casually.

"Well done!" Heron slapped Daylen's back this time. "Courting the lead hunter's daughter, aren't you?"

I hadn't thought about it that way before. But I suppose courting me was an honor to Daylen. I didn't like the idea. I wanted to think Daylen liked me for me, not because of who my father was.

"Do you think Jaria is coming back?" Heron asked. "She really is beautiful. It'd be a shame if she kept herself locked up with that old crone."

I wanted to strike him for speaking about Jaria like that but decided against it.

Instead, I laughed and hoped it didn't sound too forced. These were Daylen's friends and, soon, they'd be my friends as well. Heron was clearly the ringleader of the group, and I didn't want to upset him.

"I wouldn't mind Jaria for a suitor, you know," Heron said.

"Who's your suitor now?" I asked, looking for a female to show up behind him, but nobody did.

"Odd one out this time," he said with a shrug. "Bad luck, but the females outnumber the males. We drew straws, and I lost."

"I'm sorry," I said.

"Don't worry," he said. "Jaria isn't courting anyone, is she?"

"I'm not sure she can…" I began but stopped because Heron wasn't listening to me. I wasn't offended as he walked to talk to someone else. I was done talking to him too.

I spent the next hour meandering through the group. I already knew almost everyone, but we had been children then. I wasn't surprised when I discovered Daylen's group was composed of the adolescent males from the hunting group and their suitors for the season.

I wasn't sure what I thought of them, but Daylen made it easy to be part of their group. The inclusion was a gift after Jaria's rejection.

We played games and laughed. We danced under the light of the moon. I learned what the others had been doing since becoming adolescents. Our group lingered long after the bonfire became embers and most of the village had gone to bed.

Slowly, almost unwillingly, our group drifted apart for sleep. Daylen pulled me aside and asked, "Do you want to see the stars from Northridge?"

I was sorely tempted. It was a romantic idea, the type of thing I didn't know I wanted until today. It was a fantasy that I both wanted and feared.

I stifled a yawn. "It's been a long day," I said.

"We reset the traps," he said, nodding in agreement. "We could go check them tomorrow."

"That sounds nice," I said, surprised that I meant it. "Maybe trapping can become our thing."

"I like that," he said. "Someone needs to manage them. Why not us?"

I smiled my approval before turning to walk back to my house. Now that we were parted, I regretted calling it a night.

I turned to look back at him and saw the way Daylen was admiring me. He had a look of longing that I had never expected to see in a suitor. He missed me already.

I practically skipped home, my heart dancing in my chest. I'd enjoy having a suitor more than I thought.

Chapter 6

I began trapping with Daylen every morning. It had to be early so we could finish before he met the other hunters for the day, but having time alone with him was worth the effort.

Soon, those mornings with Daylen became the best part of my day. It became a familiar and welcomed activity. Before long, I was capable of resetting the snares on my own, and it became less of an educational opportunity, but a source of companionship.

With Daylen's encouragement, I began spending my afternoons in the tannery. Tanning was messy business and not traditionally female work, but it was acceptable. I wasn't fascinated by it, but it was thrilling to do something controversial.

Pa and Stepma were happy with the changes Daylen had brought to our household. Maybe we had proven to be a nontraditional couple with our morning trapping, but we were providing for the village, and that gave my parents pride.

It wasn't long before my family invited Daylen over for dinner and encouraged me to eat with his family as well. Bryson liked having Daylen around, and Daylen already treated him like a younger brother. Sometimes Bryson joined us on our morning trapping run or Daylen would play-fight with Bryson, allowing him to build the skills necessary to become a hunter.

I would visit Daylen's sister Maime after finishing my work in the tannery. I brought her teas and herbs that Stepma had mixed and talk with her while she prepared her new house for her coming child.

When we had been younger, Jaria and I had scoffed at the lives of adults. How meaningless all their work seemed. We had wondered why the hunters were allowed to fight when nobody else was. But now that I could see my place in the society, I began to stop questioning it. Now that Daylen had entered my life, I could finally see myself becoming an adult inside the village.

Even the pendant lost its strangeness. Despite never wearing a necklace before, the stone felt like a natural part of me.

Just as I overlooked the stone, I tried to forget what had happened at the bonfire. My new life was far too exciting to be distracted by false visions from the Fae or an old friend who had returned from the dead.

The evenings were the hardest. Like most adolescents, I'd spend them in the community house.

The community house was a large building crowded with tables and benches. It provided a place to be outside our homes. Usually, the adolescents would linger at the tables on one side while the childless adults used the others.

There, I'd gather with Daylen and his friends. I was unsure if I liked the company, but Daylen liked them. Hanging out with his friends was a small compromise for me to make since I didn't have any close friends of my own since Jaria left.

One night in late summer, I walked into the community house and was surprised to see Jaria was there

Jaria sat at one of the tables, both part of the group and separate from it at the same time. I couldn't imagine what she was doing there but decided not to ask. Maybe she was apprenticed to the Mother, but she was our age. She was allowed to be here.

I walked to the counter and poured a glass of sweet drink. I sat across from Jaria and offered her the cup.

"No, thanks." She handed it back to me.

"Why are you here?" I asked.

Jaria rolled her eyes. It was a familiar gesture. "Mother Gazina thought I was spending too much time cooped up with her."

I laughed. "Probably true."

She gave me a dark look, and I wanted to take back my joke and laughter.

Then she laughed. It was shrill and different from the laugh I remembered from our childhood, but I'd take it. Maybe our old friendship was in the past, but we could find a way forward.

Heron looked at Jaria, stunned by her laughter. Then he pointed to her, making her the center of the group's attention.

"To Jaria!" He lifted his cup towards her. "The most beautiful among us and the least accessible. May I find a way to reach your heart!" As he toasted, he leaned towards her and kissed her directly on the lips.

Cries of encouragement and laughter filled the room. As for Jaria, she sat still, her face blank.

He reached his hand forward to touch her fur, a caress.

With lightning movement, she grabbed his wrist.

"Don't touch me," she said quietly.

"What?" He asked.

"Don't touch me." As she spoke, her training as a Mother became obvious. Her speech carried force. Her voice resonated, stronger than what should've been possible. The hall grew quiet.

After a moment, Kadee, one of the adults, stood up. The adults allowed us to get rowdy, but they had their limits.

Kadee towered over Heron. "What happened?"

"I kissed Jaria," Heron said.

"But I didn't want to be kissed," Jaria said.

Kadee looked at both of them like this squabble was beneath her. "If he tries that again, let me know. I'll handle it."

Heron was trying to put on a brave face—he was a hunter after all—but Kadee was terrifying. His leg trembled, giving him away.

"It won't happen again," he said.

Satisfied, Kadee returned to the other side of the hall. She sat, facing us.

There was movement in the corner of my vision. I turned towards it to see Jaria running from the hall. She was using Kadee as a distraction to get away.

I chased after her.

"I'm so sorry, Jaria!" I shouted as I followed her from the building. "Heron really is terrible."

"Go away." She didn't even turn to look at me.

"All I want to do is help you!" I grabbed her shoulder, hoping she'd turn around and talk. "I can't help you if you won't tell me what happened to you."

She stopped walking, turned, and grabbed my wrist the same way she had caught Heron's earlier. Her grip was painful.

"Don't you dare touch me either," she said. Her voice was low, threatening. She was serious. Jaria dropped my wrist and kept walking.

I waited, praying she'd feel regret and turn around. She didn't. "Fine, I'll stop trying to be your friend," I muttered under my breath.

She twisted around and pointed to my pendant. "I can't be your friend, not since that happened."

Then she was gone, disappearing into the forest.

I considered chasing after her, desperate to understand what she meant, but then my wrist ached where she had grabbed it. It would be pointless to chase her, Jaria wouldn't give me answers.

I returned to the community house, my stomach turning on itself. I wished Jaria hadn't shown up tonight, I had been doing an excellent job forgetting about her.

I sat with the others while Heron made another joke.

"I'm so handsome that she can't stand to kiss me. She'd rather be with that ugly crone of a Mother," Heron said. He went on, and everyone laughed. Previously, I'd gone along with Heron, but this time Jaria was the center of his fun.

I considered saying something, speaking up in her defense. I even opened my mouth to speak but then remembered how she had walked away. She didn't want my help. We weren't friends. Jaria had made that clear.

Then Daylen laughed at Heron's joke.

"Was that funny to you?" I asked, my voice cutting. Anger burned within me, despite my best attempts to stop caring.

"The idea that Heron's handsome, yeah? He's the ugliest of us!" The others laughed at Daylen's joke.

I shook my head. "None of this is funny." I stood to walk out of the community hall. Maybe I should've left with Jaria. Now I was the one making a scene.

Daylen followed me and grabbed my hand. "What do you mean?"

"All of this—your little hangout—it's stupid."

He frowned. "They're my friends."

"Then why do they laugh at my friend?"

"Is Jaria really your friend?" he asked.

"I don't know!" Everything was tangled in my head. "I think it's best if I do the trapping by myself tomorrow."

Daylen frowned. "Alice, I'm sorry. I didn't mean to offend you. I thought—I mean—I like you."

That was the first time he had said he liked me. I considered my next words carefully, but it was hard, my anger remained hot.

"I might like you too," I said, "but…I don't know anymore."

"Fine," He replied, letting go of my hand. It may have been my imagination, but I thought his voice had trembled with hurt.

I nodded, not trusting myself to speak, and left.

Chapter 7

I left the house early the next morning, successfully avoiding Stepma and Pa.

They had seen I was upset when I had come home the night before, but I'd feigned exhaustion and gone straight to bed. With my brain spinning in frustration, it had taken me forever to fall asleep, but it was better than facing their interrogation.

I didn't even understand why I was so upset. Yes, Heron had been rude to Jaria, but I wasn't only angry with him. This ran far deeper than that.

I had acted like a fool in front of my peers, and I was embarrassed to see them again. I had already lost Jaria, could I even make a new friend? I knew I was angry with myself.

That still wasn't all of it. I was somehow disappointed I hadn't made a bigger scene. I should have faced Heron directly.

I wasn't thrilled with how I'd acted, but I didn't know how I wanted to behave either.

Daylen—this whole suitorship—confused me. Once, I'd promised myself not to take a mate. I'd wanted to be like

Mother Gazina or Kadee and become an independent female in our village.

Since meeting Daylen, that plan was falling apart. Now my sense of identity was crumbling within me, and I was losing my sense of self. How did I want to face the world?

That was the real reason I was angry at Daylen. It wasn't that he hadn't stood up for Jaria, it was that his mere existence as my suitor was breaking my perspective.

I no longer knew who I was, and he was someone I could blame.

I was still angry the next morning. I stormed to Northridge like I'd told Daylen I'd do. With each step, my frustration with Daylen escalated, growing in my heart.

I reached the traps and discovered they were empty. It made my mood even worse. I'd have to return to the village empty-handed. Everyone would see that Daylen wasn't with me and assume it was my fault the traps were empty. Alice: the female, the child, someone useless without her suitor.

When I discovered the last trap was also empty, I threw the game bag onto the ground and left it there.

I ran, racing my way across the village. I had to go somewhere safe. I began running towards my tree. My muscles shifted under me, adrenaline pumping as I moved. I'd do anything to escape my frustration.

The anger chased me. I ran faster.

When I reached the tree, I practically leapt onto it, clawing my way up, desperate to be within its protection, its branches, its leaves. If peace of mind existed, it had to be in the safety of that tree.

I found a seat on one of the larger branches. It held my weight without creaking.

My heart pounded. My breathing was harsh, but I savored the rush of endorphins coursing through me.

I didn't feel great, but I did feel better. This tree was familiar. It was a comforting object in a shifting landscape.

Here, I could avoid my family, friends, and suitor. If nobody could help me understand what was happening, then it was best for me to be alone.

I watched the sun while it moved higher in the sky. The morning fog cleared, and sunlight began to warm my fur.

I fiddled with the stone around my neck and let my thoughts drift to the day I had received it. What did the Fae want with me? What had they done with Ma?

The stone didn't give me answers, so I made up my own. Maybe Ma saw something she shouldn't have, or perhaps the Fae were evil and sometimes needed a Bigfoot sacrifice? I allowed my imagination to wander.

A strange breeze passed through the tree…

My nostrils flared as a familiar scent wafted my direction. I sat taller.

The scent was familiar, pulling me back to that morning of the Solstice. It was a human smell, the scent of the boy who carried a bow but didn't know how to hunt.

I scanned the ground, searching for him and his bumbling movement. I was satisfied to find him several trees away. He even carried that silly bow and, given how he handled it, hadn't learned a single thing about how to use it.

It's a compound bow, something within me said. The device remained strange, but suddenly, I understood how it worked. In the right hands, this was a powerful weapon.

I squinted, turning my head, reassuring myself that the boundary was protecting me.

But I couldn't find the boundary. I expanded my search to discover that the golden perimeter had wandered, revealing my tree. It had happened before, but never near a human.

I was exposed.

"By the Fae," I cursed. How could my day get any worse? What sort of stupid game were the Fae playing with me? Maybe this was how my ma vanished, and I was going to be just like her.

"Who's there?" the boy called out. His voice trembled with fear as he prepared his bow. "Show yourself, I'm armed."

I looked down, his bow was pointed towards my tree. I was hidden by the branches, but he knew someone was there.

My heart raced as I debated my limited options. I could hide or fight. Maybe I could run, but if the Fae really wanted me revealed, I couldn't run far enough.

It was no coincidence that it was the same human as before. The Fae wanted something from him. Or from us.

I jumped from the tree.

As I fell, there was a flash of blinding light. It startled me and ruined my landing. My chest burned where the crystal pendant touched my fur.

The pendant hadn't done anything since the Solstice. But now, of all times, it decided to do something. I hoped that it was a good sign and not something that was going to get me killed.

The human boy stared at me as I walked towards him. Of course, he stared, I was a Bigfoot.

"Who are you?" he asked. "I've never seen you around."

Who am I? The correct question should have been *what* am I.

But the boy didn't respond like I intimidated him. He was scared of the forest and of his own bow, but he didn't seem afraid of me.

"I'm Alice," I said.

"Mark." He reached his hand out, asking for a gesture that I suddenly knew as a *handshake*.

I moved my hand forward to grab his and was shocked to discover that my hand had…changed.

My fur had vanished and was replaced by bare flesh. My hand looked…

Human.

My gaze traveled up my arm and to my chest. I studied my legs.

I was undeniably human. My usually furry body was covered with clothes. I wiggled my toes, awkward in their shoes.

This had to be some sort of illusion, but it felt so real.

I glanced at my pendant, resting on top of the shirt. It hung, uselessly, like a piece of jewelry.

The boy grabbed my hand and shook it, "Nice to meet you, Alice."

The skin-to-skin contact was strange. There was no fur between us. It felt unnatural, intimate, and gross.

"Where are you from?" he asked.

"Around," I said. "You?"

"I'm from Piner. I live in town."

I'd never heard of Piner but nodded like I understood.

"What brings you here?" I asked. "Nobody ever comes here, except me."

He raised the bow into the air. "Hunting."

I laughed. I didn't mean to, but I couldn't help myself. The boy didn't know how to hunt. He moved too noisily.

"Why are you laughing?" He asked.

"It's just…"

"Go on," he insisted. "I've been practicing. I can hit the target every time. But I've no luck in the forest. My dad thinks it's hilarious too. So—tell me—what's the joke?"

I hesitated. I didn't want to embarrass him, but he asked for the truth. "Your movement is terrible. You scare every living thing away."

"And you can walk better?" he asked.

"Yes." Then I showed him, crossing several feet away and back soundlessly. Thankfully, this transformed body moved like me. "Like that," I said.

"Yeah, I'm moving like that." He followed my path, creating a racket of cracking branches.

"You're doing it wrong."

"What am I doing wrong, exactly?"

I considered it but didn't know what to say. It was like explaining how to breathe. I moved that way, I'd learned to walk without noise when I was a child.

"Didn't your pa teach you how to walk right when you were a kid?" I asked.

He looked at me strangely. "I learned to walk. Yeah."

"They didn't do a very good job."

"Did your parents seriously teach you stealth as a toddler?"

I didn't know what to say. Of course, Pa had taken his time teaching me to walk silently. Humans didn't?

"Alice!" someone shouted my name.

The sound was distorted, but my heart jumped when I realized it was Daylen. He had come looking for me! He had even thought to check my tree. My anger with him dissipated with the thought of actually seeing him.

Daylen shouted again, its sound garbled by the perimeter, "Alice, are you here?"

I looked at the human boy. By some Fae miracle, he hadn't noticed the shouting. For that matter, I was surprised to discover I could hear anything through the boundary.

"Listen, I've got to go," I said.

"Wait! Where are you from, really? Can I see you again?"

I shook my head. "I've got to go."

I left him, retreating to the safety of the boundary.

As I passed through it, there was another flash of light and spark of heat. The crystal pendant had reacted a second time.

I looked at my arm and was relieved to discover that my flesh was transformed. I looked like myself again. I was covered with fur, and the clothing had disappeared.

I didn't feel any different, it was like nothing had changed. Yet…my whole world was transformed. I could look like a human. I'd spent my life believing I could never leave my village, but now, by this power, I had freedom.

The possibilities this presented were endless.

I was relieved when I saw Daylen crest the hill. He hadn't seen my transformation. My secret was safe.

"Alice!" He ran forward and pulled me into his arms. We had barely touched before, but now—his contact, his heat, the smell of him—it was intoxicating.

How could I have been so angry with Daylen? Only hours ago, I'd wanted to end our relationship, but now I was comforted by his presence.

"I'm glad I found you." He paused for breath. "I've been searching for you all morning. I checked the traps but saw the game bag on the ground. I was so worried. I ran to your house, and your stepma said I should look here."

I wanted to say something mean. I'd been so angry with Daylen, but now that he was here my frustration was gone.

"I'm sorry that I laughed at Heron's joke," he said. Our eyes met, and his darted away. "I'm serious. It took me a while to understand that he was cruel to Jaria. That's who he is, and I'm used to it."

I glared at Daylen.

"But that doesn't make it okay," he continued. "The truth is that I'm not comfortable standing up to him."

I pursed my lips, folded my arms, and stepped back from him. I wanted to judge him the way I condemned myself for not standing up for her.

"Alice," he said. "I'm sorry. I want to stand up to Heron more, but it might take some time. I can become the Bigfoot you deserve. I think you're really interesting and beautiful."

"You think I'm beautiful?" I asked, stunned.

"Of course," he said. "You're Alice."

Excited, I leapt up and kissed him on the cheek. I'd never kissed a boy before. It was strange, and I hoped that I'd done it right.

I pulled back in disbelief with what I'd done.

He grinned. "So, you'll forgive me?" he asked.

I nodded.

Then he opened his arms and pulled me into his embrace. It was warm, tucked inside his fur. Despite my changing perspective, I felt safe with Daylen.

In his arms, forgiveness and forgetfulness were easy. There would be time to think about the crystal pendant. I needed to consider the human boy who had seen me at the boundary, but it could wait.

For now, in this moment, there was only space for Daylen.

Chapter 8

Daylen and I stayed tucked among the trees for as long as we dared. While I was with him, my mind was at ease, but I had no idea what I'd feel once we were apart.

But I couldn't stop the sun from rising higher. The hunting party would be training today, and Daylen was already running late.

We had to go our different ways.

I followed Daylen back to town and pretended to go to work in the tannery. But once we were separated, I ran back to my house. Stepma was gone, which was perfect. I needed to borrow something of hers.

I walked up to the washing bowl and looked to the wall behind it. There, hanging from a nail, was Stepma's mirror. The wooden back had been carved with birds and flowers. Stepma would never approve of me taking it into the woods, but she wouldn't find out.

I took the mirror back to my tree and waited at the boundary. I was relieved to discover that the golden line had returned to its usual position. My tree was safely inside the Bigfoot bounds.

I hesitated at the edge. I didn't really want to cross, but there was information on the other side. I'd been given this pendant and needed to know what could be done with it.

I took a steadying breath and stepped across the boundary. It rippled gold like sunlight as I touched it.

Then, like before, there was a flash of light. I felt heat on my chest where the pendant touched me. Once I was on the other side, I studied my hands. Like before, they were human, hairless. I rubbed them together and felt their smoothness. I touched my face, it was soft too.

Cautiously, I closed my eyes. I lifted the mirror in front of my face.

I reopened them to meet my reflection. Human eyes stared back at me.

My eye color was unchanged, rich and creamy, but that was the only thing familiar about the face staring back at me.

Fleshy cheeks showed on my face while spiky dark hair sprung from the top of my head. My face was strangely angular without fur.

Like before, I was wearing clothes. Some sort of blue pants made from a heavy fabric and a light white shirt. I wore shoes that covered my entire foot.

As I considered my clothes, words began to stream into my mind, filling it with information I'd never been told. I was wearing *jeans*, a *V-neck*, and *sneakers*.

I didn't understand where the knowledge had come from but trusted its accuracy. These were the human words for what I was wearing.

I took a long breath and walked back across the boundary. The stone reacted like it had before: light and heat. I looked back in the mirror, satisfied to see I looked like myself again.

I crossed back and transformed again. I looked like a human. I looked around me, checking I was alone.

Then I lifted the necklace from my chest. As the pendant came away, the hair on my face returned, and I transformed back to myself.

For that moment, I was a Bigfoot outside the perimeter. A sense of nakedness and vulnerability overwhelmed me.

Panicked, I yanked the pendant back on, relieved when I became human once again.

"So, that's how it works," a voice said nearby.

Startled, I nearly dropped Stepma's mirror.

I spun to look around, but nobody was there.

Then, suddenly, Jaria was standing beside me. I knew she hadn't been there before, it was like she had appeared from nowhere. She was removing a necklace from her own neck— the one with a pendant similar to mine that she had been wearing at her wrist.

She smirked, then slid her own necklace back on. She vanished.

"Jaria, wait!" I yelled. "What's going on?"

She laughed. Her giggle made me uncomfortable.

I crossed the boundary and retreated to safety.

"Where are you going?" Jaria asked, "I thought we could play."

"I'm getting away from you."

I glanced at my arm, confirmed I was Bigfoot again, and then began walking to the village. There was enough time to work in the tannery.

"Wait, Alice!" Jaria called after me.

I turned around, towards where she had been standing.

Jaria appeared, pulling off the necklace. She was standing near me, inside the boundary. She began to wrap the leather strap around her wrist and didn't turn invisible.

"Your's works inside the boundary too?" I began to wonder how long she had been watching Daylen and me.

"Yes," she said.

"Do you use it to spy on people?"

"No!" she protested, but then continued. "Unless I need to. Don't worry. You and Daylen are too boring for that."

I couldn't remember her being this irritating back when we had been friends. I wanted to walk away again. Yet…I lingered.

I longed to fix what was broken between us.

Jaria was a little older than me, and I'd known her my whole life. She had lived near me and had six siblings. Their house was crowded, so Ma would invite Jaria over to play with me.

Our friendship was straightforward when we were children. But even then, Jaria always had the strangest, most fantastical, ideas for the games we could play. We could play at being humans, maybe the Fae, or something made up like centaurs.

Once Ma disappeared, Jaria came over to my house while Pa worked. We didn't play, but she'd sit with me. She had been grieving too.

When Jaria had disappeared—overnight and without warning—her disappearance had ripped a hole in my life.

I'd longed to have her back, and here she was.

"You said we can't be friends," I began. "But can you tell me what is happening? I won't tell anyone."

Jaria shifted her foot, moving dirt.

"At least tell me why we have these." I pointed to my pendant.

"The Fae have been busier than normal," Jaria said.

"The Fae? How do you know that?"

"I've seen them. Many times."

"Is that where you went?" I asked. "When you disappeared, you were with the Fae?"

She nodded. "There. And other, more human, places. I've been preparing."

"Preparing for what?" I asked.

She pointed at my pendant. "For that."

This was getting creepy. I didn't trust the Fae and wasn't sure I wanted to be involved. But I had to know more. This pendant gave me freedom I'd never dreamed of. It brought me closer to my ma.

"And these crystals are…What exactly?" I asked.

"They're gifts."

I scoffed. "Strange gifts. What do the Fae want with us?"

Jaria shook her head, not answering.

"Why did my ma have a pendant like this?" I asked. It was my most important question. "Jaria, she was like a mother to you. If you know anything, you've got to tell me."

"I don't have to tell you anything." Jaria swallowed, uncomfortable with her own words. "But I don't know what happened to your ma."

I lifted the pendant from my neck and held it in front of me. I tried to come up with something clever to say. I wanted to toss it at Jaria's feet.

But I couldn't.

Instead, I stood there, hand outstretched. I couldn't throw this possibility away. I wanted to know things, and this power gave me a way to learn.

"Okay," I said, pulling the crystal back to my chest. "I'll go along with this. For now."

"Perfect," Jaria said. "Tomorrow after trapping with Daylen don't go to the tannery. Instead, come by the Mother's house. I will take you to meet the humans."

Then she put on her own necklace and vanished.

I'd do as she said. Not because I was obedient, but because this was an opportunity I couldn't say no to.

Chapter 9

The next morning, I failed to contain my excitement while Daylen and I checked and reset the traps. Everything in my life was transforming, but instead of feeling overwhelmed, today I felt alive.

I longed for Daylen's touch, seeking his electricity at every opportunity. Now that our affection was physical, I felt like a lovesick girl and was desperate to keep his attention on me.

But my enthusiasm was for more than Daylen and our kisses.

I had the power to leave the village. Jaria had said we would go on our first adventure today, and I couldn't wait to see what lay beyond my home. Only my insatiable affection for Daylen kept me from leaving the village the moment I woke up.

It was a glorious morning. The traps were full, Daylen was charming, and I was daydreaming of adventure.

Once we left our game at the cookhouse, Daylen swept me into a final embrace. When we separated, Daylen walked towards the hunting pavilion, while I approached the tannery.

However, as soon as he turned the corner, I changed my direction. I walked to Mother Gazina's house instead. It was the second time in two days that I'd deceived him. A part of me did feel guilty, but I didn't know how to explain.

I opened the door to the Mother's house but hesitated before stepping into the structure.

The Mother's house was at the center of the village, an unusual location for a home, but critical for its purpose. But this wasn't like any other home in the village. The Crux was kept here.

There was a large front room that housed the Crux, while the Mother and Jaria lived in the backrooms.

The front room was large and dedicated to the Fae. It was a public space and available to the entire village, but I'd avoided it and only entered when Stepma had business with Mother Gazina.

I wasn't sure why I avoided the house. It didn't seem bad, but there was something uncomfortable about the Crux. There was the way my hair rose, spine shivered, and nose twitched when I was around it.

I stood at the door, hoping that Jaria might step forward to greet me so I wouldn't have to go in.

The Crux was in the center of the room, resting on a table. It was in the shape of a pyramid and about the size of my two fists together. It was made from a material I'd never seen elsewhere. Nothing I knew of was that bright of a white. If I dared to come at night, I suspected that the Crux could glow.

Circles of firm cushions surrounded the Crux. When Stepma came here, she'd sit on one of them and gaze into the stone. I'd sit next to her, uncomfortable. When I asked why she wanted to come here, she encouraged me to meditate with her. I chose not to.

A chair, the closest thing I'd ever seen to a throne, was against the back wall. Mother Gazina's chair. It was majestic and cut from a boulder. A smaller rock-made stool had been placed next to it.

The room was empty.

"Hello?" I asked from the door.

I heard shuffling from the rooms beyond. Jaria stepped into the front space and walked towards me.

"Good morning," she said. "Let's get to work."

Jaria walked, storming ahead, while I followed. We didn't talk. Sometimes Jaria would glance my way to check that I was near, but she didn't talk with me.

Finally, as we approached the boundary, I spoke up. "So, are you going to tell me what we're doing?"

"You're going into the human town," she said. "I've spent a long time preparing everything for you, so don't mess it up."

When we reached the boundary, she removed the pendant from her wrist and began to shift it to her neck.

"Wait!" I shouted. "Don't go."

Jaria sniffed. "I'm not going anywhere. This is my disguise, I can't turn human like you." She made it sound like that should've been obvious.

I shrugged and crossed the boundary, transforming into my human form.

"Where are you?" I asked Jaria.

"I'm right here," she said. It was strange to hear her voice without seeing her. "Keep walking. We'll move down the hill, cross a stream, and up a rise. Then you'll see it. I had to build it out of sight from the village."

"Build…it?" I asked. "What is it?"

Jaria didn't respond.

I walked, following her directions. From the top of the next rise, it was clear what she had been talking about.

There was a small house, similar to those built inside the village but different. There was something human about the house. Bigfoot houses were simple cabins, but this structure had a front *patio* with a door and a *one-car garage.*

New concepts flooded my mind. Not just *patio* and *garage*, but *electricity* and *running water* too.

"You built this?" I asked.

"With some Fae assistance," Jaria said. "But I designed it."

"What is it?" I asked.

"Our new home."

"But I've got a home," I said, "and a suitor."

"You'll need somewhere here too. A human address, a place with Internet and electricity. A place for homework."

"Internet? Homework?" I asked, the strange meaning to the words coming to me. I wasn't sure if I was thrilled to be part of this adventure anymore.

The front door opened. I could almost imagine Jaria standing there, beckoning me in. Even though she barely talked, I could sense her excitement in showing me this place. She was proud of this.

I followed after her. There was one central room. It was large, rectangular, and brightly lit. A fireplace on the side was the only decor that reminded me of who I was. A TV was positioned above it. I stood between the fireplace and a couch. A ladder rose to a loft above, while a small kitchen lined one corner and a desk stood in the opposite one.

I climbed into the loft and found two beds.

"Are you expecting us to live here?" I asked, feeling like I was talking to myself.

"Sometimes it'll be necessary," Jaria said.

I didn't ask her to elaborate.

"Come over here," Jaria said, opening a side door.

The door opened into the garage. I looked at the car. After a lifetime of living on my feet, the fact that humans had cars to help them travel long distances was inconceivable to me.

"Tour's over," Jaria said. "About time we got you to camp."

"Camp?" I asked.

"Just get in the car." A door opened, and I sat on the seat.

"Do you know how to drive this thing?" I asked.

Another car door opened beside me, and I heard Jaria settle into the back seat. "No, but that does."

I looked at the seat next to me. A woman, a mannequin that appeared nearly human, acknowledged me with a stiff wave.

"Who are you?" I asked it.

"It can't respond," Jaria said. "It's an enchantment. But it can act as your driver until you're 16 and can drive yourself to school."

"16?"

"Speaking of, there's a purse at your feet. It has an ID card and some money," she said. I glanced at the object but didn't pick it up.

When Jaria said she had been preparing for me, I hadn't expected her plans to be so elaborate. Some fraction of me felt touched that she had cared so much for my needs. But I didn't understand why.

"So, are we going to sit in here or go somewhere?" I asked.

"You're right," Jaria said as the enchanted mannequin turned a key and the car roared to life. "It's time to go."

The car left the garage and drove down a long driveway. It joined a narrow road that took us further downhill.

As we drove, I heard the sound of air rushing by. I watched how fast we were moving, marveling at the speed. We were moving in a way that my people, confined inside our boundary, would never be able to do.

I studied the changing landscape as it transformed from wild green plant life into pastures and farmland. The transition, in some ways, wasn't unlike what I saw in the village. However, in other ways, there was something strange in the way humans used the land. The treatment of the land was mechanical like it was separated from the earth it was on.

The narrow road connected to the main highway. As I marveled at its construction, words like *pavement* and *concrete* came to my mind. I sensed how permanent the material was compared to the dirt paths that I knew.

Soon, we passed a road sign that proclaimed: "Welcome to Piner, Entrance to the Mountains, Population 10,273."

Piner. I'd heard of this place. Mark, the boy from the boundary, said he was from here. I wondered if I'd see him, but given that there were over ten thousand people in Piner, it seemed unlikely.

I couldn't imagine that this one town contained over ten thousand people. My own village was several times smaller than that. And, to think, this was only one town. How many humans were there?

Billions. The knowledge came to me the same way the other words had. There were billions of humans on this planet. And the Earth was much bigger, much more diverse, than this little piece of land I was on. I added the fact to the growing list of information I couldn't comprehend.

The only evidence I had that all this was possible was the neighborhood springing up around me. The houses were huge. Four Bigfoot houses could have fit inside one of them, yet I understood that each house only contained one family of humans.

Eventually, we reached the town center. A series of small shops lined the street. There was a coffee shop, a diner, and a library. The town hall was here too.

The car drove forward until it reached a large brick building. A sign proclaimed that it was "Piner High School, Home of the Lumberjacks." Under it, a rolling marquee said: "Enjoy your summer!"

Until today, I'd never heard of high school. Now I was overwhelmed by all the strange impressions I had of it. I knew it was an institution where questions could be answered. I realized it was a place where adolescents were crowded together and encouraged to get along.

The car stopped in the drop-off zone in front of the school.

"What are we doing here?" I asked Jaria.

"Taking you to camp," she replied. "Now get out of the car and head in."

I opened the door and stepped outside. "Have a great day, honey!" the Fae enchantment said robotically. I closed the door before it could say anything further.

The main entrance was easy to identify, and I opened the door and stepped into a large hallway. There was a desk in the lobby, and a man sitting behind it.

A human. I'd come so far but hadn't interacted with a single one of them. I told myself to act natural, not even sure what that meant.

"Are you here for the volleyball camp?" he asked.

I nodded. I knew I was here for some sort of camp.

"The gym is straight ahead, they're getting started now."

The man turned back to the computer in front of him.

I nodded and, pretending this was the most normal thing, walked forward. I approached the gym, looked around, and debated walking elsewhere.

But then the man looked up at me. "Yep, that's the right one. Go on."

I didn't really have a choice without appearing suspicious. I walked through the door.

Chapter 10

From the moment I stepped into the gym, my ears were bombarded by the sound of squeaking tennis shoes. Girls, maybe my age, ran around the perimeter of the gym. Three large nets were strung up, dividing the gym into two.

Volleyball nets. I scanned the gym and quickly found a cart full of *volleyballs.* I knew volleyball was some sort of game, but whatever power was giving me information couldn't tell me how it was played.

Two women stood in the center of the gym. One whistled as the girls ran past. She was angular and tall. The coach evaluated each of the girls as they ran, muttering something to the woman with a clipboard.

The woman with the clipboard was shorter. She was dense and muscular.

I stood at the door, unsure of what to do next. I couldn't believe I had made it this far into the human world without really having to interact with anyone. But soon, I'd have to do something.

While I hesitated, the girls ran past me. Now that they were near, I realized how much shorter everyone else was compared to me. I knew Bigfoots were taller than humans, but it was uncomfortable to accept how the transformation hadn't changed that.

Fear stuck in my throat. I may look human, but I was different. Would my height make it easy for them to see through the illusion? Would they know I was Bigfoot?

I had never been tall before. By Bigfoot standards, I was the shorter side of average.

The girls stared at me when they passed. Human or Bigfoot, I could recognize the look of female appraisal. I straightened my spine to my full height, trying to seem intimidating.

But as they looked me over, I discovered intimidation wasn't a human approach. The girl who ran at the front of the pack muttered something to the girls next to her, both of them laughed. I hoped that it wasn't about me but suspected it was.

The shorter woman walked up to me. "And what's your name?" she asked.

"Alice," I said without thinking.

She looked at her clipboard. "Alice Turner?"

Sure, why not. "Yes, that's me."

"Excellent, glad you showed up. Go get dressed and join the others in warm-up."

I looked down at my shoes, not understanding what I should do.

The woman peered over her clipboard, evaluating my full height. "And it says here you're a freshman?"

I nodded. I knew a freshman was about fourteen years old. I could be a freshman.

"Your gear is in locker 111. This is the combination."

She handed me a slip of paper and returned to the center of the gym. The other girls were now spread throughout the gym. They began a series of stretches.

I walked into the locker room, found locker 111, and entered the combination. As I opened the door, a note fluttered out. It read:

Dear Alice Turner,

Please don't disappoint us.

Sincerely,
Your Faery Godparents

The paper vanished as soon as I finished reading it.

I sighed and pulled the clothing from the locker. Shorts and shirt in the same fashion as the other girls. I changed into the clothes, my fingers struggling to handle the unfamiliar materials. Clothing was strange after a lifetime without it.

I left the gym, catching my reflection as I did. I really did look human. It was hard to believe that the human in the mirror was me. I pulled the pendant out from under my shirt so that it hung above my jersey. That looked a little better. It was something to remind me of who I really was.

I nodded to my reflection as if I could encourage myself and stepped back into the gymnasium.

"Okay ladies," the tall, angular woman shouted. "Gather round."

The girls shuffled to stand around her. I ran to join the back of the mob.

The girl who had been leading the pack turned towards me. I wasn't sure what human beauty looked like, but I guessed she had it.

"Look at you," she said to me. "You might be tall, but if you're part of my team, you can't be late."

A few girls nearby laughed.

Maybe I didn't understand humans, but I knew bullies. I ignored them. I already knew I was stronger than humans.

"Welcome to Piner High's volleyball camp," the angular woman said. "I'm Coach Nelson, and this is my assistant, Coach Higgins. A few words before we get started. First, this camp is your tryout for the varsity and junior varsity teams. As you know, school starts next week. Our first match is that Thursday."

The girls around me shifted. Camp had barely started, but the Coach's excitement for the season was infectious.

"A great season starts now," Coach Nelson continued. "I know camp can be tiring, but we need to have a solid week of training.

"Coach Higgins and I'll be watching you this week and will post rosters for both teams on Friday morning. We've 24 spots to fill, and there are about 40 of you. The competition will be tight, so best of luck to everyone."

Varsity and *junior varsity* teams. I could define what they were, but I didn't quite understand what it meant. Regardless, I could smell the tension in the air. Every girl here wanted to be one of the 24 who made the two teams.

"Now that you're warmed up," the coach continued. "Let's get started with some drills. Count yourselves off into six groups." Then she pointed to the courts where each number should gather.

We counted off. I was disappointed to realize I was in the same group as the bossy girl who had called me out for being late for a volleyball camp that I didn't know I was attending.

"We'll start with serving drills," Coach Nelson said. Then she continued to describe a series of complex movements. I wasn't sure what a serve was.

"Lexi, can you demonstrate?" Coach Nelson tossed one of the volleyballs towards the girl I was trying to avoid.

The girl, Lexi, caught the ball and threw it into the air. As it fell towards the ground, she hit it with her other hand. The ball flew up and over the net, smacking against the floor on the other side.

"Excellent. Thanks, Lexi." Coach Nelson handed a second ball to the girl and proceeded to talk through each step of the motion with Lexi as her example. Lexi moved gracefully, confident in her place as the example athlete.

I frowned. This girl really was talented, and she knew it too.

"All right, girls, let's get started," Coach Nelson said.

Lexi served a second time. The movement was fluid, like a dance. I tried not to look impressed.

Lexi smiled and moved to the back of the line. I watched as the other girls served, trying to understand the movement.

Soon, I was near the front of the line. I watched as the girl in front of me served differently than Lexi had shown us. She held the ball in one hand and used her other forearm to hit the ball over the net. It was a method that didn't require hitting a falling ball.

"If you're ever going to make the team, you need to have an overhand serve," Lexi said.

The girl shrugged.

"Then again," Lexi continued. "You're so short that you don't have a prayer."

The girl took her place in the back of the line.

It was my turn. I picked up the ball, my first time ever handling a volleyball. It felt good to hold, and I gripped it in the fingers of one hand.

"Giant girl has giant hands," Lexi taunted.

I wanted to throw the ball directly at Lexi, but instead, I tossed the ball into the air. I prepared to hit the ball as it fell.

Then…I missed.

The ball was already on the ground by the time I was ready to strike.

Lexi laughed, and other girls joined her.

I picked up the ball and served the same way the last girl had. An underhand serve. It was easier than hitting a moving target.

—*bam*—

My forearm struck the ball with such force that it stung my skin. The ball soared towards the ceiling. It smacked down on the other side of the net. Maybe it wasn't an attractive serve, but I was pleased.

"Guess I don't know my strength," I said, walking to the back of the line. Within, my stomach turned. What in the world had I gotten myself in to?

The girl who had first done the underhand serve turned to look at me. "I'm Payton," she said. As much as I disliked Lexi already, she had been right: this girl was short. I looked down to meet her eyes.

"Alice," I said.

"You're a freshman?" Payton asked. "I mean, most of the older girls were on the team last year, but I didn't recognize you."

"Yeah, a freshman."

"Me too," Payton said. "I've only been able to play volleyball in gym class. I wasn't able to join a seasonal club." She looked to the ground like she was ashamed of that. "But school sports are free, you know? Thought I might as well try and join the team, maybe I could make JV."

Payton talked a lot. I liked that.

"Actually, I have a confession," I said. "I don't know anything about volleyball. My godparents signed me up for this without asking."

"Oh, wow. I knew I hadn't seen you before, which middle school did you go to? I went to Grayson."

"I just got here," I said, the lie feeling close enough to the truth. "So, what do you know about this overhead serve? I want to try again."

"It takes practice. I've done it before, but I'm not consistent. I didn't want to embarrass myself."

By now, we had reached the front of the line. Payton paused for a moment as she considered the ball. Then she threw it into the air and struck it. She landed the hit but angled it too low. The ball hit the ground before passing over the net.

Lexi laughed, but Payton smiled my way, shrugged, and jogged to the end of the line.

It was my turn, and I threw the ball into the air. I'd been watching the other girls and mimicked the way they positioned their hips and walked into the swing.

At that moment, I allowed my reflexes to take over. I didn't know this sport, but I understood my body. I had the grace necessary to do this. I swung forward and whacked the ball.

—*crack*—

I made contact. The ball flew up and forward, landing cleanly on the other side of the net. It wasn't beautiful like Lexi's serve, but it was a vast improvement.

I walked to the end of the line, and Payton offered her hand.

"High five?" she asked.

I clapped my palm against hers. The sound was satisfying—even in the noisy gym. The feel of flesh against flesh made me uncomfortable.

We served several more rounds before Coach Nelson asked everyone to stop.

"Passing drills! Pair up!" she shouted.

I glanced towards Payton, and she nodded. I didn't understand this sport, but maybe, with Payton by my side, I could learn.

And, perhaps, I could even enjoy becoming Alice Turner, a freshman at Piner High School.

Chapter 11

Coach Nelson continued the day by leading us through a series of passing drills. By working one-on-one with Payton, I finally had the chance to feel the volleyball and learn how it responded to my touch.

Each time I made contact with the ball, the more natural it felt. I enjoyed the way my body moved to accomplish the drills—the way I had to be agile and responsive.

In the Bigfoot village, only males were trained to move this much for their work. Females needed to be useful with their hands, dexterous but not athletic. My preference for bodywork had made me uncomfortable my entire life, and it was liberating to play with the volleyball.

Before long, Payton and I were well matched. We found a rhythm with the ball moving between us. She showed me the tricks she knew, and I practiced them, optimizing them for my own body. I experimented with my own ideas, and she gave me feedback.

Time slipped from me as we played and, before I knew it, Coach Nelson was shouting, "Great job, ladies. Take 15 minutes to do what you need. Bathroom, water, snack. We'll put everyone into teams for scrimmage. We have time for a few quick games before lunch, then you're free to go home."

Payton pulled up the sleeve to her shirt and rubbed the sweat from her face. "Sounds great to me, I'll be right back." She ran off to the locker room.

Once she left, I realized that, besides Lexi, I didn't know anyone's name. I refused to walk up to Lexi and wasn't sure how to introduce myself like a human. I leaned against the bleachers, trying to seem casual.

Now that we would be scrimmaging, I realized I didn't understand the rules of volleyball. Soon I'd be playing a game that I didn't know. I didn't want to embarrass myself.

One of the girls from Lexi's cohort broke away from their group and walked my way. She was smiley, chipper in a way that was either annoying or endearing.

"I'm Olivia Carmichael," she said.

"Alice," I replied.

She wavered, but then started speaking, the words coming quickly once she had committed to them. "I wanted to let you know that I'm sorry that Lexi is picking on you. I'm trying to stop her, but she only respects me so far."

"So, what do you want?" I asked. I figured this girl was here on some sort of joke.

She grinned. "I want to play, I want us to have the best team we can have. Lexi can be difficult, but she is an excellent player. Anyhow, You're tall and strong. You've got potential. So, don't let Lexi ruin your game."

By now, Payton had returned.

Olivia looked at her, smiled, and said, "Well, best of luck during scrimmage." Then she turned around and rejoined the girls surrounding Lexi.

"Was that Olivia Carmichael?" Payton asked me.

"Yeah," I replied, "what about it?"

"I can't believe you were talking to her! Wow, I knew you were good, but you've impressed Olivia!"

I didn't know how to respond. There were social rules I didn't understand.

"Sorry," Payton said, "I forgot you're new here. Olivia is probably going to make team captain. She made captain last year as a junior, can you imagine? She has been on varsity since she was a freshman."

Payton made this sound important, but I had other concerns. "Can you explain the rules of volleyball?" I asked. "I've got the feeling that I'll need to understand them to scrimmage."

We spent the rest of the break with Payton explaining the rules to me. The concept was straightforward: hit the ball over the net, don't let your team drop the ball, and your team had three hits. The details muddled in my mind, but I didn't worry. This was only the first day of camp.

Coach Nelson blew her whistle for attention, then Coach Higgins listed the teams. Payton and I were separated, but at least I'd get to play with Olivia. I wished Payton good luck as I joined the other girls in my group.

Olivia set us up. Six of us on the court with one alternate. When points were scored, we would rotate so that everyone had a chance to play. Olivia gave me an alternate position, allowing me to watch before I needed to play.

First, we played Lexi's team. Lexi herself gave the first serve and nearly scored right from the start. Olivia dropped to the floor, barely returning the ball back to the air. Another player leapt forward and slapped the ball to the other side of the net. Soon, I was watching a fury of hits pushing the volleyball from one side of the net to the other.

It was amazing to watch. Some of the girls had clearly been playing together for years and shouted commands I tried to follow but could not understand.

I hated to admit it, but Lexi was incredible. She was always one step ahead of the play. She hit the ball with precision, landing it exactly where there was no one to return it. Their point.

It was my turn to step onto the court.

During my first rotation, I avoided the ball. I was too afraid of making a mistake and that I'd cause the other team to score by doing something wrong. When it came time for me to serve, I was relieved when the ball reached the other side of the net, even if it was easily deflected.

By the end of my rotation, I couldn't avoid the ball any longer. Lexi had caught on to my uncertainty and purposefully aimed the ball my direction.

I considered running, letting the return be someone else's problem, but that'd give Lexi the satisfaction of scoring.

Instead, I allowed my reflexes to take over, and without thinking, smashed the ball to the other side of the court.

Lexi managed to get under the ball. Her teammate set up a play, and then Lexi scored.

I rotated out. However, as I stepped off the court, Olivia approached me. She spoke in that thoughtful way of hers, "Alice, you should try to hit the ball a little more often. The only way you learn is by practicing."

Her words stuck with me, and during my second rotation onto the court, I began searching for opportunities to hit the ball. Sometimes I missed, and at other times I ran into my own teammates while trying to reach the right spot.

But the more I reacted, the more attuned I became to the flurry of coordination around me. I found a rhythm, a flow. Despite the crazy circumstances that had led me here, this was actually fun.

The set ended when our team lost by three points. Coach Nelson rotated Lexi's group with another, and we started a second set.

By now, my team was beginning to understand how to play together. I learned how to call out for the ball or to tell my teammates I was setting up their play. Halfway through the second game, I scored my first point. I shouted with excitement, and Olivia clapped my shoulder in congratulations.

I lost track of time. I'd played games as a child, but they hadn't been competitive. Not like this. Playing this way—with my blood pumping and endorphins surging—made me feel alive. Every time my team scored, I was eager to help it happen again.

We won that second set.

When Olivia scored the final point, I cheered with the rest of my team. By now, I knew most of them by name and, while I didn't know anything else about them, it didn't matter. What did matter was that we had learned to work together and trust each other's abilities.

Once we were done, Coach Nelson blew her whistle a final time and asked everyone to circle around her. We were a sweaty, tired group of humans.

"Great job," Coach Nelson said. "Be sure to hydrate and get some rest. I'm excited to see you all tomorrow."

We broke away, and the girls began walking to the locker room. I followed the crowd, but then I heard my name.

"Alice, can I have a word?" Coach Higgins was walking towards me.

"Yeah, what do you need?" I asked. Suddenly, the confidence I had felt with the team was fading. I wasn't part of a group anymore but an individual. I was a Bigfoot with human skin.

"I saw your files. You're new to Piner High? I know this must be quite a transition after homeschooling."

"Yeah, new to school!" I tried to smile like this was a common experience. I had no idea if it was.

"Well, let me welcome you to Piner High then. I teach social sciences. Maybe I'll be your teacher next semester."

I nodded, waiting for her to continue.

"Well, nice to meet you," she said. "Good luck with tryouts."

Then she walked away to talk with another athlete. I wondered if she was that nice to everyone. She seemed like the kind of person who would be, but I wanted to believe she had singled me out because I'd done a good job.

I'd never been good at anything in the village. I was curious and liked to know things, but that wasn't a gift. I wasn't the smartest or the best problem solver.

Yet here, playing a game with humans, I could finally do something right, something natural. I knew I belonged here, and that knowledge was both comforting and odd at the same time.

Chapter 12

I changed in the locker room as quickly as I could.

Now that the game was over, I was uncomfortably aware of the way sweat had beaded on my skin. It was strange that it wasn't absorbed into my fur. This human body was weird.

I heard the pouring of water and realized that someone had turned on the shower. Lexi stood there, naked, radiating confidence with her own body. The other girls looked at her, and someone snickered, but Lexi only glared at her. The girl apologized.

Lexi's body wasn't like any of ours, it was too perfect. If I had to guess what sexy looked like to humans, I'd think it was like Lexi.

I looked away from her, embarrassed by her exposed skin and uncomfortable with the idea of water pounding against raw flesh.

As for me, now that I didn't have fur, clothes seemed entirely necessary.

I pulled my old outfit back over my body and yanked the pendant back over my shirt. I practically ran out of the locker room before anyone tried to talk to me.

I'd been acting like a human long enough. I was already worried that I'd grown too comfortable on the court and had accidentally exposed myself. I longed to get back to the safety of my village.

As I walked from the locker room, I heard Lexi shout from the shower, "Not only does Alice act like an animal, but she has to smell like one too."

I pretended I hadn't heard and stormed from the locker room. I would show Lexi, given time. I could be just as good at this game as she was. Better, even.

I'd barely left the building when I heard someone running after me. I felt my temper rise and prepared to shout. Then I turned, it was Payton.

"Why did you leave so fast?" she asked. "I was hoping we could walk home together."

"I—I'm not comfortable in the locker room," I said.

Payton considered. "Yeah, it's weird. Especially with Lexi."

"Yeah, what was that about?"

"Showing off," Payton replied.

I laughed. I wasn't sure why it was funny, but at least I could share my opinion of Lexi with someone else.

Suddenly, I remembered the way Lexi had called me an animal. It made my breath stick in my throat. Was it really that obvious that I didn't belong?

Together, Payton and I stepped outside the school.

"I live a few blocks that way." Payton pointed the opposite direction from my village. "Do you want to meet for lunch?"

I considered her offer, despite her being a human, it was easy to be with Payton. I'd even forgotten how different we really were. It was already the easiest friendship I had experienced since...well, Jaria.

But I was also exhausted. Not only physically, but mentally.

Over the last three days, I had fought with and kissed Daylen, met Mark, discovered I could transform into a human, learned my ex-friend had built us a house, and started trying out for a high school volleyball team. It was becoming completely incomprehensible.

Suddenly, each of these changes felt like a weight. Worst of all, these were things I couldn't tell Payton. We wouldn't ever have a true friendship. I could never share who I was with her.

"Will you be here tomorrow?" I asked Payton.

"Of course! I'm going to make that JV team, remember?"

I nodded, already daydreaming about a bath in the river. "I've things I need to take care of at home, but how about lunch tomorrow?"

"That sounds great to me," she said, looking disappointed.

The car that had dropped me off that morning was now parked in front of the school. I opened the front door and settled into the seat. It felt amazing to sit.

"Welcome back," a voice said from the back seat. I couldn't see her but knew it was Jaria.

"Hope you weren't waiting long," I replied.

"I can keep myself busy," she said. "There's a lot to do."

"How was your day?" I asked.

"I'd rather hear what you thought of your day."

So, I told her what had happened. She listened, attentive, but I got the impression that she already knew most of the details.

"What did you think of Payton?" she asked as the car began to journey into the hills.

"She's nice, I like her," I replied. "Maybe I'll stay in town to have lunch with her tomorrow."

"That sounds smart, you could use a friend like her, someone to help you understand what it means to be human."

The way she talked about Payton was annoying me. It was like, to Jaria, Payton was only another human and replaceable.

But I was savoring what I had felt with Payton. We had shared the first tenuous strands of friendship, and I hadn't felt those in a long time.

I didn't say any of that to Jaria. After everything she had put me through, I couldn't expect her to understand what friendship meant to me.

Chapter 13

Stepma and Bryson arrived at home the same time as me after spending their day in the apple orchard.

During the peak season, most of the village was recruited to pick the apples, even the children. Sometimes the kids helped, and sometimes hindered, the process.

Bryson was terribly muddy. I doubted he had been helpful.

"What happened to you?" I asked my kid-brother.

"Petre and I wrestled!" He said.

Stepma frowned. "We would've stopped them, but they ran off first. They went to that alcove near the river."

I nodded. Of course, I knew the spot. It was out of sight from the adults, a perfect location for mischief.

"I won." Bryson puffed his chest. "Daylen's been teaching me things."

"Regardless," Stepma said, stopping him from entering the house, "you're muddy."

"I'll take him to the river," I said. "I wanted to clean up anyhow."

Stepma smiled, thankful. Ever since I'd begun working in the tannery, I'd been a little less helpful with Bryson. "Thanks, Alice. Are you home early from the tannery?"

I walked into the house and grabbed the bathing supplies. "Um, no, actually…"

Stepma studied me, I tried not to give anything away.

"Go take care of Bryson," she said, "but you better be ready to explain by dinner. Might as well tell Pa and me at the same time."

I nodded, sighed, and motioned for Bryson to follow me to the river. Pa wasn't going to be happy about this new arrangement with Mother Gazina.

"Guess what?" Bryson asked while we walked.

"What?" I asked.

"When I grow up, I'm going to be a hunter."

"Of course, you are," I said. The words were natural, every big sister should encourage her little brother to be a hunter. They were the most respected males in the village.

"I don't see you as much anymore," Bryson said. "I've missed having you around."

The words stung. I had tried to stay an attentive big sister but knew the truth. Since becoming an adolescent, I was spending less time with my family. This was part of growing older, I knew. I was beginning to support the village through trapping and the tannery, but I felt guilty that it took time from Bryson.

This new arrangement with Jaria wasn't going to give me any more time with my family.

"I'm getting older," I said.

"Why?" he asked. "I mean, I know you have to get older. But why does that mean I don't see you as much?"

I didn't really understand either.

"It's a hot day," I said. "If we run to the river, maybe we can get there before anyone else. That way, we can get more time on the rope swing."

I began running for the river and encouraged Bryson to chase after me. I wanted us both to forget his question.

The river wasn't only a place to clean but also somewhere to play. When the sun was hot in the sky, the riverbank became a central place for the community.

The rope swing hung from a tree near the river. It was easy to jump into the water from it.

Bryson had jumped three times before he began bothering me to try it too. I began to swing but stopped. The tree branch was giving under my weight. It was enough to remind me that I was becoming full-grown. I was too big for childish things.

So, instead, I pushed Bryson. With my help, he could jump even farther into the river. He laughed from the water, making me smile.

Bryson and me. Together. It was a familiar landscape, one where I could forget everything that was changing.

Eventually, we had to clean our fur. Once we were done, we shook the water from our bodies and laid out to dry under the sun.

"Alice?" Bryson asked.

"What?" I replied, keeping my eyes closed against the sun.

"I like Daylen," he said, considering his next words, "but I don't want you to leave and start your own family. I need you here with us."

"I like Daylen too," I said, stopping myself before I babbled everything to him. I wanted to tell him what had happened in the human town, but he wouldn't understand.

Once we were thoroughly dry, we returned to the house. Stepma chastised us for taking so long. We had been late enough that she had gone to the cookhouse to pick up dinner.

Picking up food was my responsibility. I mumbled my way through an apology and began setting the table.

"Daylen told me you had a good catch this morning," Pa said, serving stew into bowls.

"Mmhmm," I mumbled.

"Alice, what was it you were saying about your work in the tannery?" Stepma asked as she settled into her chair.

I sighed. Of course, she'd ask about this right away. "Well," I wasn't sure how to begin. "You know how Jaria is apprenticed to mother Gazina?"

"Yes," Pa stopped eating. His gaze drifted to the pendant I was wearing. He had never commented on it since the day I'd put it on, but he had to have known of its significance. After all, Ma had worn one like it.

I lifted the pendant. "The Fae gave me this at the Solstice, and I just learned what it can do."

Pa nodded for me to continue.

"I look human when I cross the boundary," I spoke quickly and then stuffed the stew into my mouth. I didn't realize how hungry I was! Maybe they wouldn't ask me questions while I was chewing.

"What do you mean?" Pa said. He was angry, that scared me. I'd expected disappointment.

Stepma rested her hand on his.

"Did the Fae ask you to do their work?" Stepma asked.

"Something like that," I replied through a mouth filled with food.

Pa stood up. "I don't care what the Fae want. No, Alice, you will not be part of their game." He began walking towards the door. "I'm going to talk with Mother Gazina."

Stepma grabbed his arm and pulled him back. They had one of their silent conversations.

Finally, she said aloud, "You can talk to Mother Gazina tomorrow morning with Alice. Going now isn't going to change anything."

Pa returned to his chair. "First thing tomorrow."

Stepma nodded, and Pa swallowed a spoonful for stew.

"You know that as an apprentice to the Mother you can't take a suitor or mate," he said. "I worked very hard to make Daylen your suitor, and you seem like a good match. Think very carefully about what you're doing."

"I am," I said. "Or trying to."

He nodded, frowned, and said, "That pendant makes you look like your ma."

I gaped. He rarely spoke of Ma. Nearly everything I knew about Ma was from my own distant memories.

"I'd hate to lose you too," Pa said.

"I'll take care," I promised him.

We returned to our stew in silence.

By all reasonable accounts, I should've been the last person to willingly enter human society. But this felt right.

I compared my potential as Alice Turner to my limited future inside the Bigfoot village. I knew it'd only been one day, and it felt silly to admit it, but I felt like I belonged to the human world better than the one I'd been born into.

The thought made me uncomfortable, but I didn't show that to Pa. He had enough to worry about.

Chapter 14

I woke the next morning without difficulty. I had wondered if I'd stay up half the night worrying, but I had been so tired that I fell asleep the moment my body hit the cot. I had been so exhausted that I didn't even go to the community house with Daylen.

But I was eager to see him that morning.

Quietly, I combed through my fur and, once presentable, walked into the living space. Pa was already awake and gnawing on jerky. I poured some water from the pitcher into a cup.

"I'll meet you outside of Mother Gazina's house after you're done trapping?" He asked.

"Yeah, sounds good." I drank the water in one gulp and grabbed a piece of jerky for myself. I headed for the front door.

"You do like him, don't you?" Pa asked.

"Who?" I asked.

"Daylen."

I bit off a piece of jerky. "I do."

"Good. Hope you have a good morning."

"Thanks," I said, leaving the house before Pa could ask any more questions.

Daylen was waiting for me. He had been at our starting point long enough to remove the trapped rabbit and begin resetting the snare.

My stomach twisted when I saw him. Guilt and desire…somehow mixed together.

It had been easier yesterday when this secret was only fun. But now I was beginning to see how elaborate the Fae's plans were.

"Alice," He set the trap aside and stepped towards me, arms extended. I fell into them, allowing him to embrace me. If there was a scent for security, it was what Daylen smelled like.

He kissed the top of my head and held me to his chest. Time stopped as my worries temporarily vanished.

I kissed his neck and then looked up so I could study his hazel eyes. My body quivered in his arms and finally relaxed when he kissed my lips.

I sighed with relief.

He pulled away, but I held him close. I didn't want the moment to pass.

"Everything okay?" he asked me.

"I think so," I lied.

"We should check the other traps," he said.

"Oh, yeah," I said.

I tried to be my usual cheerful self as we walked, but either I wasn't a good actor, or he knew me better than I thought.

"What's wrong?" he asked again.

I considered lying to him again, but said, "It's complicated."

"What's complicated?"

I hesitated, unsure how much to tell him. I knew Daylen was only my suitor, possibly temporary, but my relationship with him had always felt so natural. It was like I could tell him anything.

"I've been offered work in a different trade," I said.

"Yes?"

"It's with Mother Gazina."

"Oh," he said as if it explained everything. Maybe it did. It clarified why it was hard to talk about. Matters of the Fae were always strange.

It also let him know that our relationship could be in trouble.

He pulled away from me.

I reached for him, words tumbling from me. "I like you Daylen, I really do—this is an exciting opportunity—I don't know what to do. Pa's going to come by to talk with Mother Gazina today—everything has been happening so fast."

He considered while I caught my breath. "Isn't Jaria her apprentice? Does she need two?"

I paused, trying to figure out what to say, but didn't find any words.

"I guess," he said, "I thought we were a good match, but if you need to end this—"

I grabbed his arm. "I don't want to end this!" I couldn't imagine leaving him, not now that I needed him.

I didn't realize how attached to him I had become. Daylen was someone I could be myself around, even when my entire world was shifting.

"Okay," he said. "Let's see where this goes."

Then he turned and began walking to the next trap. He moved awkwardly, clearly disturbed.

I ran after him, shouted out, and jumped on to his back. I laughed, pretending we could end this morning like an ordinary day.

Daylen followed my lead, choosing to believe nothing had changed between us either. It was a good game of make-believe.

When we dropped the game off at the cookhouse, I glanced towards Mother Gazina's house. Pa was already standing outside of it. He was watching us.

"I'll go over with you," Daylen said.

"Thanks," I said.

We walked to him together. Daylen was bold enough to hold my hand and share his strength with me.

"Good morning sir," Daylen said to Pa.

"Morning, Daylen," Pa replied, "I'm sure Alice has told you of her…situation."

"A little, yes," Daylen said.

"Well, trust me when I tell you I'm going to get this all back under control. Don't you worry."

Daylen nodded.

"Go ahead," Pa told Daylen, "I'll see you in a few minutes."

Daylen looked back to me.

"I'll see you tonight," I told him. "Let's meet in the community house?"

"See you then." He nodded and walked towards the hunting pavilion.

I wished I could've kissed him goodbye, but I was too shy in front of Pa. Instead, I turned and pushed open the door to the Mother's house.

Mother Gazina was inside, seated on her stone throne. Jaria was there too. I had the feeling that they were waiting for us.

"Good morning, Mother." Pa walked past the Crux and took a seat on a cushion near her. I followed, hovering near the Crux. The rock was comforting in a way that it had never been before.

"Good to see you, Caiman," Mother Gazina said.

I watched Pa chew his words, surprised to see him this nervous. Eventually, he found the words he was searching for and asked, "Why do you want Alice to be with the humans?"

"It's not that I want her, or even that the Fae asked for her," Mother Gazina said. "It's her birthright."

Birthright? That was news to me.

"You expect me to trust them with Alice?" Pa said. "We still don't know what happened to Evie…I've been given the responsibility to care for Alice and this—"

"This was too be expected," Mother Gazina interrupted. "Alice has been granted a special ability. You should be honored."

"—Evie felt honored—" Pa muttered.

"This is a gift," Mother Gazina continued, speaking over him.

"—nobody can take Alice away—"

"You are not the one who gets to decide," Mother Gazina said. "Alice is."

Pa turned to me. "Alice?"

"I want this, Pa." The words were out of my mouth before I had time to think about it. "At least, I think I do."

"That's the problem!" Pa said. "She is far too young to be making a decision like this! Alice is a child!"

"I'm old enough to pick a mate!" I said. I didn't know what outcome I wanted from Pa's intrusion, but I wouldn't be treated like a child. "I can make my own choices now."

Pa's lips tightened into a line. He stood so that he towered over Mother Gazina's throne. "Alice is too young." He said it like it was final.

Mother Gazina stood. She barely reached his chest but didn't cower.

Instead, she extended her hand towards the Crux.

A ray of light extended from her fingers, connecting her to the pyramid's peak. The room began to buzz.

My chest grew warm. I looked down to see that my pendant was glowing and saw Jaria's was doing the same.

Mother Gazina began to glow as light extended from her. Her eyes turned pure white.

I stepped back from her, but Pa stood his ground.

"Do not question my authority over these matters." The Mother's voice was deeper, holding strength beyond her own body. "There are powers at work beyond your comprehension."

"At least give Alice time to make a choice," Pa said.

The Mother looked to the Crux like she was consulting it. Then, all at once, the light vanished.

"Alice will have until the next Solstice to choose her path." Mother Gazina's said, looking directly at me. "Then, Alice must either return the powers the Fae have given her and reenter regular society. Or she must embrace her role with the humans in its entirety."

Mother Gazina rested her hand to the armrest, clearly weakened by the display. Jaria helped Mother Gazina to her seat.

I waited for Pa to speak, but he didn't. Instead, he looked back towards me.

"Very well," I said. "The Winter Solstice then."

Pa rubbed his head, sighed, and nodded. He didn't like this arrangement, but he'd accept it.

I turned to Jaria. "Let's get to work?" It was the second day of volleyball camp, and I wanted to be on time.

Jaria glared at Pa while she stood. He lifted his hands and stepped back, he was no threat to the Mother. He had already gotten the best deal he could negotiate for me.

I walked out with Jaria and didn't look back at Pa. I needed him to know I was frustrated that he had interfered.

But by the time we reached the boundary, I wished I'd thanked him. Pa had bought me the time I needed to figure out what I wanted. I wished I had told him that time was the most important gift he could have given me.

Chapter 15

I arrived at the school with enough time to step into the locker room before warm-up. Changing clothes, while strange, was more comfortable the third time. It was reassuring to know I was figuring out my human body.

I ran from the locker room and fell into a jog with the other girls. Their speed was slow, and I realized I could be leading the pack. I considered passing Lexi at the front to prove to the coaches that I belonged on this team.

But then I heard my name. "Alice, hey! How are you?"

Payton ran up to me, breathing heavily.

"Hey," I said, dropping into pace next to her.

The second day of camp was similar to the day before. The first half of the morning was spent doing drills. Once again, I was placed into a group with Payton.

Payton and I were well matched. She had more experience, but I was intuitive. It was easy for us to coach each other while we did the drills. The nasty competitiveness I felt towards Lexi never manifested with Payton. She was delightful to be around.

Like the day before, we scrimmaged for the second half of the day.

Playing volleyball was harder than it had been the day before. Yesterday, I'd been thrilled to hit the ball. Today, I wanted more. I tried to score points. However, despite my best efforts, the ball never landed where I wanted it to go.

After a particularly lousy serve, I heard Lexi mutter to another girl, "Alice the Animal, eh? Big and strong, but stupid."

The other girl laughed.

The words stung. I wanted to shout and defend myself. I wanted to fight her, to beat her.

But I knew fighting wasn't the human way. I needed to blend in and chose to pretend that I hadn't heard her slur.

The next time the ball came to me, my impulses took over. I didn't aim to score, but instead targeted Lexi's face. I struck the ball with as much force as I could manage.

The ball smashed Lexi's wrists as she returned it. The sound of impact smacked in the air, but it didn't even phase her. Lexi watched while her teammate spiked the ball and scored.

Then Lexi turned to look at me. She knew what I'd tried to do. She smiled at me, like a dare, asking if that really was the best I could do.

My plan had backfired. Now more of the girls muttered the new nickname: Alice the Animal. As more girls began saying it, I began to wonder how different an animal was from a Bigfoot. Was my human act fooling anybody?

I couldn't land a good hit for the rest of the game. Every single time the ball came towards me, my heart pounded in my head and rage made my blood hot. I didn't want to win the game, I wanted to beat Lexi.

The anger wouldn't leave, and it made it impossible to find my flow. Volleyball wasn't any fun this way. The only thing stopping me from pummeling Lexi into the ground was the knowledge that doing that would definitely make everyone think I was an animal.

I wasn't human, but I had to play by their rules.

After what felt like forever, the coaches finally released us for the day. I stormed into the locker room, pulled my street clothes on, and walked right back out.

I knew Lexi would make fun of me again—calling me an animal for not showering—but, if I moved fast enough, maybe I could leave before I accidentally punched her.

"Alice, are you okay?" Payton ran after me. She hadn't even changed and was swinging her backpack over her shoulder.

I shrugged and waited until we left the building to talk. "It's Lexi. Do you know what she called me? Alice the Animal."

"I heard," Payton said, "well, that stinks. But do you still want to come to my place? We can throw a pizza in the oven, watch a movie, or something?"

I nodded absently, thankful as concepts like *pizza* and *movie* came to the forefront of my mind. Payton's proposal was interesting. I shook my hands, hoping the anger would pass soon. It was continuing to burn.

"I'm not sure I'm really in the mood for it," I said.

"It's fine," Payton's voice rose with excitement. "You need to get out of the gym and away from Lexi. Give it time."

I hesitated. The longer I thought about pizza, the hungrier I felt.

"Okay," I said.

Payton led me as we walked together a few blocks to a blue house. She walked to the front door and led me inside.

"It's a little small," Payton said, "but it's only Mom and me here. We don't need a lot—"

"It's huge!" The house was twice as big as the one I lived in with my family.

Payton laughed. "Alice, I've no idea where you come from, but it must have been somewhere really different."

I laughed too. "It really is."

She gave me a brief tour of the house, and I tried not to be impressed by a kitchen or bathroom with running water. Payton gave me a strange look when I said how impressed I was that she had her own bedroom.

I tried to act casual while she preheated the oven. Really, I was trying to understand her actions without seeming like an idiot who had never used an oven before.

"Where's your mom?" I asked.

"Working," Payton replied. "She's a manager at the grocery store."

"And your dad doesn't live here?"

"He moved to the city when Mom and Dad got divorced."

"I'm sorry," I said. Divorce did happen inside the village, but parents couldn't exactly leave the town.

Payton shrugged. "I was pretty young when it happened. I see Dad every month or so. He got remarried, and my step-mom isn't too bad. I've got a step-sister about my age, she's actually kinda cool."

"I've got a half-brother," I offered. "But he's a kid."

"What about your parents?" she asked.

I hesitated. "Ma disappeared when I was young."

"Disappeared?" Payton appeared shocked. "Like, the police never found her?"

"Yeah, something like that." I shifted the conversation. "My pa is a hunter and Stepma helps with the farming and taking care of Bryson."

I immediately wished I'd come up with a better lie.

Payton considered me for a moment before continuing, "You really do live in the forest, don't you?"

"I guess so." I was uncomfortable with the way she was looking at me…like I was too strange. "Maybe I shouldn't tell the other girls at school about that—"

"No, I think that's really cool!" Payton said. "I'd be dead in one day if I had to take care of myself in the wilderness."

"Really?"

"Yeah," Payton said. "So how did you end up at Piner High School?"

"My godparents thought it'd be a good idea. I decided to try it out."

"Wow, culture shock," Payton said.

I laughed, it was good to talk about this with someone, even if that person was a human. "Yeah, definitely."

A timer went off, and I jumped. Payton laughed. "It's pizza. Tell me you've had pizza before."

"Of course, I've had pizza before," I lied.

Payton sliced the pizza, plated it, and handed a dish to me.

I was starving and eager to eat. Pretending it was completely natural, I lifted the crust and took a bite. The pizza was hot, and the top of my mouth scorched with pain.

I forced my face into a smile and said, "Mmhmm, delicious."

I swallowed the bite, unsure if I'd really tasted it. Then I set the slice back down for it to cool before trying again.

"What movie do you want to watch?" Payton hadn't even taken her first bite, she'd already known it was too hot. I should've followed her example.

"Whatever you want." I didn't know enough about movies to know what my options even were.

"Let's see what's available," Payton took her plate over to the couch and began browsing options on a TV. I was glad she was the one using the remote, it was intimidating. Too many buttons.

"Oh, this is one of my favorites." Payton played a trailer for an adventure movie. It starred a woman who had to save humanity from aliens.

"Looks good," I said.

Payton pressed play.

By now the pizza was cool enough to eat. I tried a second bite and was happy to discover that I actually liked it. There were so many more ingredients than the simple stews I was used to at home.

"That's good pizza," I said.

"It's nothing. Stuff mom brings home from the store." Payton seemed surprised that I'd compliment the food, but honestly, it was one of the yummiest things I'd eaten in my entire life.

I was hungry and finished the pizza before the opening credits were over.

"Do you want another slice?" Payton asked.

"No thanks," I said.

"Well, I'm full, so if you want this, take it. We can always make another one." Payton set the slice on the coffee table in front of us.

I tried to resist but grabbed the slice before the first scene of the movie had ended.

"Thank you," I said. I wanted to tell Payton I appreciated her, not just the pizza I wanted to let her know I saw her as …a friend?

"No problem," Payton said.

I had so many questions but didn't want to make it awkward. I focused on the movie instead.

The movie was unlike anything I'd seen before. I'd grown up with stories, the mothers would tell them to the children, and my ma had known the best ones.

But the movie wasn't meant for children. There was violence I'd never seen before, even if the heroine was supposed to be hunting down aliens, plenty of humans were killed in the process. That much blood made me uncomfortable, but Payton got up, made some popcorn, and handed me a bowl.

I did like the protagonist, she was a fighter. She wouldn't let Lexi boss her around.

But it made me ache to think of the way the heroine had handled the aliens. The aliens were big and threatening. Yes, they had destroyed some buildings and killed some humans, but the protagonist never once imagined that they had a reason to do that. The plot just assumed that aliens were bad and needed to be destroyed.

It made me uncomfortable. What would happen if the humans met Bigfoots? Would the humans think we were threatening too? We didn't have weapons like the humans did. Any confrontation would be one-sided.

What if I were exposed? Would I be captured as a specimen? I shivered. I didn't want to think about that.

Fortunately, fatigue from the volleyball camp began settling in, and the movie grew compelling. It eased my worrying.

By the time the credits were rolling, I'd sunk deep into the couch. My tummy was full of pizza and popcorn. I was getting sleepy.

"What did you think?" Payton asked.

"I've never seen anything like it," I said.

"Yeah, I know. I like it, but kind of wish it had a better romantic interest."

"Yeah, romantic interests," I said to say something.

"Have you ever had a boyfriend?" Payton asked.

I thought of Daylen. He was my suitor, but was he my boyfriend? My face must have given me away.

"You have!" Payton accused.

"I guess so. It isn't your normal relationship." I said, hoping she didn't ask too many more questions. I couldn't imagine explaining Bigfoot courtship to Payton.

"You're still seeing him?" Payton asked. "What's his name."

"Daylen."

Payton was bouncing with excitement. "Have you kissed him? Does he live around here?"

I looked away when she asked about kissing. It wasn't against the rules for suitors to kiss, but my attraction to Daylen ran deeper than I was comfortable with. Daylen could ruin everything I was trying to create for Alice Turner.

"I don't want to talk about him," I said.

"Um, okay." Payton sat down, disappointed.

"But maybe later," I said, glad to see Payton perk up. "I really like him but…" How could I describe any of this to Payton?

"What?" She waited for me to continue.

"I like Daylen a lot, but I'm not sure our relationship is meant to be." I searched for the words to say, Payton was eager to listen. "It's hard to explain, but I have to give up something important to stay with Daylen."

"Sounds confusing," Payton said.

"It is…but I've got time to think about it."

Payton had listened to me. It was the most amazing thing anyone could do for me. Jaria didn't pay attention unless it suited her own agenda. And my family expected me to have answers for them and was frustrated when I was confused.

It seemed strange that I could talk to Payton about my problem. Yet Payton, even with her human experiences, could understand me. She listened better than anyone else had.

The doorbell rang.

Payton opened the front door. Nobody was standing outside, but a car honked from the driveway. It was the car Jaria used to take me to school.

"Is that your family?" Payton asked.

"Say yes," a voice whispered in my ear. Jaria.

I looked at Payton. "Yeah, that's my godmother. Listen, I've had a really good time, but looks like I've got to go."

"I had a good time too," Payton said.

I walked towards the car, feeling strange. It was like our conversation had been cut too short.

"Do you want to come over tomorrow?" Payton asked.

I turned to Payton, grinned, and said, "Yeah, I'd like that."

"Let's go," Jaria muttered to me.

"Bye!" Payton said.

"See you tomorrow," I replied.

Chapter 16

"Did you have a good time with your new friend?" Jaria asked as we rode back to the Bigfoot village. Maybe it was my imagination, but I thought I heard metal to her voice as she asked about Payton.

"Yeah, Payton's pretty great," I said.

"That's...wonderful," she said. Her tone became dispassionate as she continued. "The Fae were hoping you'd make a friend here. They need you to blend in, act human, and if Payton is too dense to realize—"

"Payton's not dense!" I said. I couldn't believe Jaria didn't like Payton.

"You made plenty of mistakes today. It's better for everyone if she doesn't realize you don't belong."

I sighed and leaned into the seat.

"Calling your pa a hunter?" Jaria continued. "That's nonsense to a human. They don't hunt for food, they farm it. Hunting is a sport, not a profession."

I began to turn around, preparing to stare her down while we talked. But Jaria remained invisible, and the motion felt useless. "What was I supposed to say? I'm sure you've got tons of ideas."

"I do," Jaria replied. "After all, I've been studying for this."

"And I'm supposed to know everything on day two? How do you know what I told Payton anyhow? Do you spy on me, are you invisible when I'm acting human?"

"Sometimes," Jaria admitted.

"That's disturbing." I found the idea of someone, especially Jaria, watching me terribly uncomfortable. "Why don't you leave me alone?"

"It's my job to make sure you're safe," Jaria said.

"No reason to stalk me."

Jaria sighed louder than was necessary and didn't respond.

I wanted to believe she was jealous that my friendship with Payton had developed quickly and easily. Maybe I was hopeful, but I liked pretending Jaria wanted to be friends. If watching Payton and me together made her jealous, I didn't mind.

The mannequin driver continued to take us from the town.

"You're the one who can look human," Jaria spoke quietly.

"What do you mean?" I asked.

"I'm able to be invisible. I can observe humans, but can't be with them. I left my family for two years so that you could pretend to be human. You get to be the center of everything."

"You're jealous!" I realized.

"No, I'm not jealous—not of you."

"Liar."

"Fine," Jaria said. "Maybe I wish I could look human. I can't understand why I worked for two years to be in the back seat of this operation. Meanwhile, you're the one bumbling around hitting volleyballs. You get to make friends, eat pizza, and watch movies."

"If that's how you feel," I began to pull the pendant from over my head. "You do this, not me."

"Don't do that!" Jaria shouted. I felt something icy, like mist, pass through my wrist. The sensation was strange, was that what Jaria's touch felt like? "We're not inside the perimeter yet, do you want someone to see you?"

She was right. I released the pendant, and it fell back to my chest. I knew I'd overreacted, but if giving up the crystal would've given me our old friendship, I would do it.

The mannequin drove the car up the driveway and parked it in the garage.

Stepping into Jaria's house now that I'd been inside Payton's showed me how unusual it was for a human home too. Jaria had worked to create something half-human and half-Bigfoot.

Jaria had done an excellent job. This was a house where both Alice Turner and Alice-the-Bigfoot could be comfortable.

I opened the front door and felt the strange cold sensation a second time. It was definitely Jaria. I wished I could see her, I hated having this conversation with someone invisible.

"I'm sorry," I said. "I didn't know what this meant to you. I guess I should've realized…The house is amazing, by the way. A perfect mix of human and Bigfoot."

I hoped that had made her smile. She was always proud of how clever she was.

We began to walk towards the village.

"How could you have known," she said. "I never told you. I never told anybody."

"Two years?" I asked. It was inconceivable. It was one thing to pretend to be human, but at least I could interact with others. The idea of spending two years invisible…it sounded isolating. "Was it awful?"

"In some ways, it has been the most fascinating adventure of my life. But do you know what the worst of it is? I can't interact with the world properly when I'm invisible. I can move inanimate objects if I want to, but I can't touch another living being. It's like I'm denied my own existence." She hesitated. "I spent some of that time with the Fae too."

"Where—what are they?"

"You know I can't tell you that," she said, her tone returning to its normal iciness. "Maybe one day they'll let you visit them, but until then you've got me."

"Oh." I really hoped to see the Fae sooner than later, I had so many questions.

When we crossed the boundary. My human form vanished as Jaria appeared next to me. I shook my body, encouraging my fur to lay correctly. It felt wonderful to be back in my own body.

Jaria began wrapping her pendant to her wrist. She flexed her fingers, enjoying the movement.

"Thanks," I said.

"Thanks for what?" Jaria asked.

"For being my friend."

"I'm not your friend. I'm the—"

"Intermediary, I know," I said. "You connect me to the Fae, I get it. But can we be friends too?"

Jaria looked me over, she seemed exhausted. "I'd like to be your friend again, but I don't know if I can."

"Why not?"

"Alice, the job will always come first."

"We're playing at high school!" I said. It sounded ridiculous out loud. "I'm trying to join an adolescent's sports team. If this were so important, the adults would be the ones doing it."

"They needed someone who can look human," Jaria said. "You're able to do that."

"Why can I do it?" I asked, "Mother Gazina talked about a birthright this morning."

Jaria stopped walking. "Alice, I actually don't know what your pa and Mother Gazina meant by that."

"Oh," I said, surprised. I thought Jaria knew everything. "Why do they need someone at all?"

"The future of the Bigfoot people depends on it."

I laughed. "On me playing volleyball? No."

"This isn't just about looking human," Jaria said. "This is about learning how to be one of them. We need someone who really understands the human perspective. The Fae don't need a Bigfoot, and they don't need a human. They need someone who can be both."

"Why?" I asked but recalled the movie I'd watched with Payton. If the aliens had been able to relate to the humans, would they have been destroyed? Maybe, maybe not.

Jaria waved me away. She was done talking. I wanted to bother her again, to see if she'd let anything else slip.

I didn't. She seemed too tired. This, whatever we were doing, was wearing her out.

Instead, I considered comforting her, offering my support. But I held back.

We weren't friends. We couldn't become friends. The job would always come first, like a wall between us. I'd tried to ignore it but suspected this would be better for both of us if I stopped resisting. It was best if I came to terms with the truth: our friendship was over.

The understanding didn't make me angry—I was past anger—but grief still choked within me as we parted ways for the night.

Chapter 17

I was relieved when my parents finally excused me after dinner. It'd been an awkward meal, and I couldn't imagine spending another moment inside the house.

Pa had been making references to Daylen all night, either how good of a hunter he was or how great of a couple we could become.

Meanwhile, Stepma tried to ask me what I wanted to do: Did I want to become an apprentice to the Mother or not? What were my feelings on the matter?

She meant well, but her questions were like an interrogation. I didn't know what I wanted and was pretty sure I wouldn't figure it out at the dinner table. Besides, since I didn't need to make a decision right now, what did it matter?

Meanwhile, poor Bryson was frustrated that he couldn't quite understand why everyone was upset.

A part of me was nervous to see Daylen later that evening. There was a fraction of me that believed our relationship was doomed and suggested I should end our suitorship before we grew any more attached.

But every time I convinced myself that ending our relationship was the only way forward, I couldn't imagine him with anyone else. How would I handle it if he picked his next suitor for his mate? I wasn't ready for everything to be over between us.

I entered the community house, and my heart leapt when I saw Daylen was already there. He was seated at one of the long tables, surrounded by his friends. He held a cup of dice as part of the game they were playing.

Daylen grinned when he saw me and waved for me to sit next to him. I did. Daylen lifted his arm and wrapped it around my shoulder. I nuzzled into his warm fur.

After a day of constant reminders of how tall of a human I was, it was a relief to feel normal. Daylen welcomed me precisely as I was.

I sat next to Daylen while he finished the game. Sometimes I'd glance at his dice and suggest something, but for the first time all evening, my mind was quiet.

"How are you?" he asked when the game was over. "Your Pa didn't seem happy after his meeting with Mother Gazina. I hope you aren't as grumpy as he was."

My peacefulness waned. I enjoyed being with Daylen, but talking about this was ruining the moment.

"What happened with Mother Gazina?" he asked.

"Pa didn't get what he wanted," I replied.

"Did you get what you wanted?"

"I don't know. Maybe."

He hesitated, considering something.

Then he stood up, offered me his hand, and helped me to my feet. He pulled me to standing, leading me from the community hall. I blushed as others looked to us—holding hands in public—but I didn't drop his grip.

"Where are we going?" I asked.

"We're going to make a fire," he replied.

A fire? I laughed. All this had begun at a bonfire. But he had an intriguing glimmer in his eye, so I followed him from the hall.

We walked to the hilltop where the Solstice was celebrated. It was a public space, but unpopular in the heat of summer. I gathered kindling while he browsed the stack of logs stored nearby.

While Daylen lit the fire, I laid out on one of the benches. My entire body was sore, and stretching out felt terrific. It allowed my mind to quiet again. It was late twilight, and I studied the moonless sky. A few stars began to shine against the darkening horizon. It was warm, and I treasured the cool breeze that ruffled my fur.

Soon, I heard the crackling fire and smelled the smoke. I rolled to my side and studied the small dancing flames. Daylen stood nearby, prodding his work as needed, encouraging the flicker to transform into fire.

I'm not sure how long I studied the fire while Daylen tended it. Long enough for Daylen to add larger logs and the flames to grow.

Daylen sat beside me, and I stirred to sit up. He touched my shoulder and helped me lie back down with my head resting in his lap. He smelled of pine, soap, and ash. Real smells. Much more enchanting than human perfumes. This was the scent of my people.

I relaxed into him and shut my eyes to memorize this beautiful moment. I wanted to hold on to this forever.

"I've been thinking more about what happened the other night," he said. "With Heron."

"Oh?" I hadn't expected the conversation to start this way. So much had happened since then.

"Did you know that Heron and I are neighbors?" he asked.

I didn't. I shook my head.

"Heron and I grew up playing together, practically brothers. But…" He chewed his lip. "Heron turned out better than me."

My hair rose at the thought. I rotated into a seated position so I could look Daylen in the eye.

"You're way better than Heron," I said.

"Not as a hunter." He looked away, ashamed. "Heron has this instinct. He knows how to get what he wants. He is the strongest, and everyone likes him. He's always been that way, even when we were kids."

Because I helped raise Bryson, I knew how hunters were trained. Technically prospective hunters weren't chosen until adolescence, but even at this age, Bryson knew his strength would mean everything. If Heron had always been talented, even as a child, what would that have meant for Daylen?

"I'm always comparing myself to Heron. But I can't beat him." Daylen rammed his fist into his opposite hand. "He's always stronger than me. Faster. More popular."

I rested my hand over Daylen's fist. "That doesn't make him a good person. You're a good person. It's something he's not."

"I know that," he said. "You can say that, but…I want to beat him. I need to be better than him at something."

I thought to the other night, how Daylen had laughed with the rest when Heron made fun of Jaria. Even if he hadn't found Heron funny, he couldn't risk standing out from the pack.

"When I'm around you," Daylen continued, "I don't feel the need to impress anyone. That sounds crazy, I know. You're my suitor. If there's anyone I should want to impress, it should be you…"

He finally met my eyes, I waited.

"I'm free to be who I am around you," he said. "I like that."

"I like who I am around you too," I admitted.

The fire crackled as we paused.

Then my confession tumbled from my mouth: "This pendant makes it possible for me to look human."

Now that I'd started talking, I couldn't stop. I explained everything that had happened in the last few days. How I'd discovered my power, traveled into the town, and begun joining a human sports team. I told him that I started school next week.

"Jaria says the Fae want me to learn human culture." I continued. "This isn't about a game—or even getting an education—the Fae need someone who knows what it's like to be human."

Nobody had forbidden me from telling anyone what was happening, but that wasn't necessary. I understood the need for secrecy.

If everyone knew I was infiltrating the humans on the Fae's request, many of my people would become angry or fearful. It could ruin our peaceful community. It was the type of secret Bigfoots trusted the Mother to keep.

But if I was going to do this, I needed help. I'd only known Daylen as a suitor for a few months, but there was nobody I trusted more.

Only now that I had confessed, I worried I'd been selfish. Now Daylen was responsible for my secret too.

"You can't tell anyone else," I said. "I mean Pa knows, but I doubt he'll talk about it. I don't think it would be good for the village if everyone knew."

He laughed at the thought. "Obviously this is a secret. But, really, you can look human?"

"Yes!" I stood and pulled his hands. "Let's go to the boundary, I'll show you."

Another couple was coming towards the fire. Daylen considered them and stood.

"Okay, let's go," Daylen said, following after me.

We walked, hand in hand. Once we were out of earshot from the village, I told Daylen about volleyball and tried to explain the rules. I talked about Payton and how much I liked her.

I told him about Lexi.

"I don't know why," I said, "but I want her to like me. It's like I have to prove to her that I belong on this team."

"Sounds like Heron," Daylen replied.

I hadn't realized that. If Lexi could be liked because of her volleyball skills, Heron could be popular for his strength. And I'd only met Lexi. Daylen had spent his whole life comparing himself to Heron.

"I don't even know why I care," I said.

"And I don't know why I care about Heron," Daylen replied.

We reached the boundary and stood next to my favorite tree. I paused before crossing the boundary. Could Daylen still care for me after witnessing what I could become?

I inhaled and stepped forward.

Without fail, my chest burned hot, and light flashed. I transformed. I looked down to discover I was wearing a knee-length floral dress. Skinny straps came up over my shoulder. The human interpretations of *cute*, *beautiful*, and *sexy* all occurred to me.

My desire to impress Daylen had come through in my transformation. I began to worry if Daylen would see me more attractive this way. Did I really want him to find the human version of me sexy?

"By the Fae," Daylen muttered. "You look—somehow you look like you only—"

"Human," I said.

"Exactly." He reached his hand towards the boundary. I reached for him and allowed our hands to touch. For a moment, barely distinguishable, I felt his furry hand in my fleshy one.

Then I crossed the perimeter, transforming back into myself. His hand felt right in my fur-covered one.

He lifted our joint hands and led me through a spin. He admired me as I turned.

"Alice, you're one beautiful Bigfoot. Maybe the humans will call you an animal, but that's because you're wild. But this," —he gestured towards all of me— "this is the best version of you."

I smiled, memorizing his words. I wanted to repeat them to myself that evening. I fell into his embrace, so happy that Pa had chosen him as my suitor.

Then a dread thought returned to my mind, unwelcome.

"What happens next?" I asked him.

"What do you mean?" he replied.

"I can't both help the Fae and be with you at the same time."

"You have until Winter Solstice to decide?" he said.

"I do," I replied.

"Then let's wait and see what happens." He said. Then he kissed me, squarely on the mouth. I stepped back in surprise but smiled when I realized this was all right, uncertainty and all.

"Is this okay?" he asked.

"Yes," I said, kissing him back.

And it would be okay. I needed it to be.

Chapter 18

The rest of the week blurred together. I shifted between the different parts of my life. In the mornings, I checked the traps with Daylen. I spent my days playing volleyball against Lexi and watching movies with Payton. Every evening, I saw my family for dinner before joining the other adolescents in the community house.

When I was a child, I'd spent my life in the company of Stepma and Bryson. The transition into adolescence should've been enough to manage, but now I was exploring humanity too. Every day was filled with new information and experiences. I'd never felt so alive nor had I ever been so exhausted each night.

Then, somehow, it was Friday. The final day of volleyball camp.

"Do you think you'll make the team?" Jaria asked during our drive to school. She didn't always accompany me anymore since the driver could take me wherever I needed to go without her. I had the feeling she actually wanted to talk with me. Or spy on me.

"I don't know if I'll make the team." I felt uncomfortable with how much Jaria knew about my life without me telling her. "You're the one who hangs out with the Fae. Can't they tell the future? Do you know if I'll make the team?"

"The Fae don't work like that," she replied.

"How does it work then?"

"Do you really want to talk about transcognitive communication? Or the aggregation of beings that can cross manifest?" She was using big words to push me away from the subject.

"Kind of. What did all that mean?" I said.

Jaria didn't reply, ending the conversation.

I hadn't given much thought to whether or not I'd be on the team. I hoped I would. Strange as the week had been, I knew I wanted to be on the volleyball team. If I was going to begin this high school experience, I'd rather not be alone.

The car stopped in front of the school, and I stepped out.

"Bye," Jaria said as I closed the door.

When I stepped into the gym, I was surprised to discover how quiet it was. Everyone spoke softer than usual as they lingered with their closest friends.

The coaches remained in their office, and everyone knew without saying it aloud that they were finalizing the rosters. I joined Payton, who was standing with other girls we had played with that week.

Only Lexi and her followers seemed confident, Olivia included. Then again, they had reason to be secure. Those girls played together in the off-season and were almost guaranteed spots on the varsity team.

The coaches stepped from their office. Coach Nelson walked with a piece of paper in her hand.

Coach Higgins spoke first.

"As I'm sure you've guessed, we are about to read out the names of the players who made the varsity and junior varsity teams. I know this can be an emotional moment, and that's okay. Tryouts are tough, and the fact that you're here says you dared to accept the possibility you won't make the team. So, before we read these names, I want everyone to take a moment to congratulate their neighbor for being here."

My heart was pounding loudly in my chest, growing more uncomfortable by the second. But I found the strength to look at Payton. She appeared as nervous as I felt. We smiled.

"Good job," I said. My voice was low, rough with anxiety. I cleared my throat.

Payton could only nod.

I heard Lexi's crooning laughter from across the crowd and ignored it.

Coach Nelson coughed, and the hiss of conversation died. "This year's varsity team will be led by co-captains Olivia Carmichael and Lexi Normandy." There was light applause, but nobody was surprised. Coach Nelson continued to read the remaining ten players who would be on the varsity team.

I held my breath while she called each name, counting on my fingers until there was only one player left to name. She hadn't called my name yet. I hadn't expected to be on the varsity team, but I had hoped to make it.

"Quinn Carter," Coach Nelson announced as the last player on the varsity team.

I watched as Lexi clapped Quinn on the back. Quinn was a freshman like me, but Lexi and Quinn were close despite the age gap. They had known each other for years and had played in the same club. Quinn had become Lexi's shadow, and Lexi liked having someone listen to her.

The tension within me relaxed. I didn't make varsity. That was okay, I wasn't sure I wanted to play with them anyhow.

"Congrats to our varsity players," Coach Nelson said. "Now for the junior varsity team."

I clenched my fist. Only twelve more names remained. I glanced to Payton, she had closed her eyes and hugged her hands to her chest. She wanted this so badly, I longed for the power to make Payton part of my team.

"Alice Turner," Coach Nelson said. That was me, right? I wanted her to repeat it, to be sure, but she had already moved on to the next name.

"Congrats," Payton said quietly, somehow sincere despite her nervousness.

I realized Coach Nelson had named me first for junior varsity. That meant I'd almost made varsity. Almost. Except for Quinn Carter.

Instead of feeling happy, I was suddenly jealous. If it hadn't been for Quinn, maybe I would've made varsity. She had spent the week lingering in Lexi's wake like a bee was drawn to a flower. It was disgusting. I could do so much better than her.

Payton hadn't been called yet. I'd lost track of how many names were left, but Coach Nelson continued calling them.

Payton was holding her breath. I tapped my fingers against my thigh. I needed Payton on my team, I couldn't imagine starting high school without her by my side.

"And Payton Appleton," Coach Nelson said, looking up from her paper. "That's it, ladies. Now, Captains, start warm-ups with the varsity and JV teams while I have a word with everyone left."

I dared to look at Payton. Her eyes were bright, glossy with tears that hadn't fallen. She was smiling like she wanted to laugh.

"Let's go," I nodded towards the region where the other players were beginning to congregate. "There is less than a week until our first game."

Grinning, she wiped her hands against her eyes. "Yeah, let's go."

Her happiness was infectious and helped ebb my anger with Quinn. I reminded myself that I didn't want to play with Lexi. Instead, I'd get to play with girls I actually liked.

"Ladies!" Olivia shouted to the group of twenty-three women around her. "We'll run laps then work on some drills."

Then Lexi shouted over Olivia. "Let's stretch first. Windmill those arms!" She began a countdown.

Olivia frowned but joined in the countdown that Lexi had started. She shouted, showing the team that Lexi had her support.

Payton and I followed suit. I glanced towards Quinn again where she stood in Lexi's shadow. Then I looked back to Payton, her grin was infectious. Maybe I hadn't made the varsity team, but I had Payton by my side.

Chapter 19

That first day of JV practice became my favorite day of the whole week. Not only did I know that I was on the team, but I knew I'd share the experience with Payton. I was relieved and played my best.

Under Coach Higgin's instruction, the JV team broke into two smaller groups and began to scrimmage. She had divided us well, and our volleys were exciting.

I spiked a ball, forcing it down on the other side of the net. My team cheered, but Ellie, one of my new teammates, complained to her neighbor.

"Alice is so tall, it isn't fair. She really is an animal," Ellie said.

My face grew red. This was my new team, and it didn't have Lexi on it. I belonged here—Bigfoot and all—my body was human. Maybe I was taller than the other girls but had only learned the game that week.

Fortunately, I didn't have to respond. Another of my new teammates spoke out, "It's great that she's tall, it'll help our team win."

The other girls muttered in agreement. Ellie didn't seem satisfied, but most of my teammates did. They might not like playing against someone of my height, but we weren't competing anymore.

We continued to scrimmage, rotating players to both sides of the court. While we had been playing in teams all week, this was the first time I knew this would become my team for a full season.

I studied the others as they trained with me. We explored how to play our strengths and defend our weaknesses. Through the course of the practice, I gained my teammates' respect. By the time we left for the locker room, I had built confidence inside my human skin.

While the others showered, I changed clothes as quickly as I could. My flesh made me uncomfortable enough, and the idea of getting my skin wet was nauseating.

"Dang animal," Lexi called after me when I left. "That Alice sure has to smell!"

The varsity girls giggled.

"Don't!" I heard Olivia say when I stepped from the locker room. I hovered, at the door and out of sight, curious what would happen next.

"Don't what?" Lexi asked.

"She's our teammate, Lexi. Don't treat her like that." Olivia's voice quieted the longer she spoke.

Lexi laughed. "Why do you protect that girl?"

I couldn't hear Olivia respond over the sound of the water. Maybe she hadn't spoken at all.

I turned to see Payton standing beside me at the exit. She shrugged her shoulders to tell me it didn't matter what Olivia and Lexi thought. They might be our captains, but they weren't our teammates.

I wanted to return to the locker room and defend myself but knew Payton was right. There wasn't anything I could say that could fix this. There was only performance. Lexi would have to respect me when I was the best player on the court. It was as simple as that.

While we walked to Payton's house, she described a few movies we could watch that afternoon. I couldn't get enough of her films. They were mesmerizing and nothing like the stories I'd heard growing up. The stories were more complex than those told in the village. My favorites featured heroines who saved the day.

I didn't know I was starving for stories until the films began to feed me. I couldn't get enough of it, and Payton loved sharing them with me.

We stepped into Payton's house and walked straight for the kitchen to make our lunch.

I was startled to discover a woman was already there. She was reading a book while seated on a barstool.

"Mom," Payton said, surprised. "You're home."

The woman, Payton's mom, set her book down and looked up at her daughter. "Wade needed to trade shifts at the last minute." She walked over to the stove and began heating a pan. "Hope that's alright."

Payton nodded.

"This means I'll be working tomorrow night," she continued. "Sorry baby, we'll have to reschedule."

"It's okay, Mom," Payton blushed when she was called *baby*, but I had the sense she wouldn't have minded if they had been alone.

"Anyhow, I thought I could cook lunch now that camp is done, but" —she took in my size— "I didn't know I was cooking for four."

I looked at the ground.

"Don't say that, Mom!" Payton said.

"Sorry," she said to me. "I was trying to joke."

"It's nice to meet you…Payton's mom." I considered her. She seemed truly apologetic.

"Tami, please," she said. "Call me Tami. I've got enough food for all of us, don't worry."

I nodded but didn't relax. Other than Coach Nelson and Coach Higgins, Tami was the first adult I'd met. Would an adult be able to see through me? Maybe she already knew I didn't belong because I was so tall.

I offered my hand to shake hers, humans seemed to like that. She shook my hand.

"It's nice to finally meet you, Alice," she said as she dropped the meat into the hot pan. "Payton has said wonderful things about you."

"Has she?" I looked to Payton who turned away.

"What are you cooking?" Payton asked. "Smells good."

"Pork chops," Tami said. "I've got potatoes and brussels sprouts in the oven. Going to make a honey-garlic pan sauce too."

"Sounds great!" Payton had already bragged to me about her mom's cooking, and my mouth began watering with excitement.

"I figured we might have something to celebrate?" Tami asked.

"Oh, right!" Payton said. "I made junior varsity."

"Glad to hear it!" Tami turned from the pork to grin at Payton and then pointed her spatula towards me. "And you?"

"Junior varsity," I said.

"Alice was called first!" Payton said. "She almost made varsity."

"Did you now?" Tami asked.

"Yes," I said. "But I think it's better this way."

"And why is that?" Tami said.

"The junior varsity girls are nicer," I said, surprised to hear myself say it out loud.

We lingered in the kitchen while Tami finished cooking. I told Tami about Lexi and the other girls, how they called me Alice the Animal.

She listened and told us a story from her days at Piner High. She had been heavier then, and the other girls had teased her relentlessly about it, calling her a pig.

"Your mom is awesome," I said when Tami excused herself to use the bathroom before we started eating.

"But…" Payton said.

"My stepma is always so worried about my baby brother. I've never been able to talk to her as easily as your ma."

"Alice, don't you get it?" Payton asked. "Don't you see what the problem is?"

I had no idea what she was talking about.

"We don't have a lot of money," Payton struggled to say the words. "Mom works at the grocery store, and dad gives her some money to help me. It's enough, but we don't have the type of money the other girls have. Mom is nice, but she can't provide for me the way other parents do. I could never play in a volleyball club like the varsity girls."

I tried to understand but failed. I nodded.

Financial differences were strange to me. Jaria had tried to explain, but it didn't make sense. In the village, everyone cared for each other. Resources were shared among the community.

My culture was completely different from anything the humans had. Jaria said economic differences led to different classes. Payton's mom was nice and could feed her, I couldn't understand why the money mattered. Jaria insisted that it did.

Payton cared that her mom made less money. It impacted her opportunities, it mattered to her. Jaria was right, somehow, but it was still difficult to grasp.

Tami returned to the kitchen and looked at our untouched plates. "I'm sure you're hungry! Dig in, no reason to wait for me."

I began to eat. The food was unlike anything I'd tasted before. Tami had added flavors and ingredients I'd never experienced. It was delicious, and I ate every single bite.

"Seconds, Alice?" Tami asked, already placing more food onto my plate.

"I'm good—" I started to say.

"Don't be shy," Tami insisted.

"Sure," I replied.

Tami finished serving the remaining food to both Payton and me, then said, "Eat up. You girls have a long season of volleyball ahead."

We watched another movie that afternoon. It featured another warrior woman. This time, it was set in a historical setting. Somewhere in a desert.

I was sleepy and began to daydream. I imagined a world where I could be a hunter, like Pa and Daylen. The heroine in the movie was able to find love. So maybe Daylen could love me as a hunter.

When Jaria came by to pick me up from Payton's house, I wanted to ask a million questions about money and how it influenced humans. I tried to ask her about the film, I didn't understand why the stories were affecting me.

But all Jaria wanted to talk about was how excited she was that I'd made the team. She kept going on about how important this would be to my human integration.

"Do you think you could advance to varsity this season?" she asked.

"No." I didn't want to think of playing on any team without Payton on it.

"You're new to the sport but placed well. Give yourself more practice, and you'll be on the varsity team in no time. There's always next year."

"I don't want to be varsity," I said.

"Is Lexi getting under your skin?"

"No," I lied.

"Don't let her bother you so much," Jaria waved her hand as if she could push Lexi aside.

I wanted to snap back at her, but that would mean admitting she was right.

Lexi did bother me. I didn't know how much longer I'd tolerate being called Alice the Animal before there would be consequences.

Chapter 20

The weekend passed quickly. I was relieved to stay inside the Bigfoot village the entire time. For two days, I didn't have to pretend to be human. After a week of throwing myself into the chaos of volleyball and relationship deadlines, I enjoyed the break from thinking about it.

With my people, I was free to be Bigfoot. That was a bigger treat than I could have imagined.

Apples were still in season, and extra help was needed with the harvest. It was an easy excuse to be with Bryson and Daylen while we picked the fruit together.

All of us would snack on an apple when we thought the others weren't watching, but nobody hesitated to call out the others if we caught them eating. It was a delicious game of hide-and-seek.

When we needed a break, Daylen would wrestle Bryson. Daylen showed Bryson how to improve his technique and would fight one-handed, allowing Bryson to win. I loved watching the two of them together. They were my boys.

Daylen would be a good father.

I blushed whenever the thought crossed my mind. I was trying to be human. I shouldn't be considering suitors, let alone a mate and children. Human girls didn't choose their mate this young, and neither should I.

However, as we worked in the fields, I watched the two of them together and knew a part of me wanted the future I thought we could share. As much as I enjoyed my gift from the Fae, I also wanted a future with Daylen.

If I began to worry about how I could ever choose between humanity and Daylen, I shut down the thoughts before they ruined a perfect weekend. Besides, I didn't have to make a decision for months.

I was avoiding the future so severely that Monday morning snuck up on me. I woke before the sun began to rise, much earlier than I had all summer.

I was meeting Daylen that morning before school. Jaria had told me I should stop my morning trapping runs. Instead, Daylen had asked if we could start our runs earlier. We could finish before I had to go to school. It meant early mornings for us, but we wanted the time together.

Trapping went smoothly that morning. It was a relief to know that we could still be us, despite my nervousness for high school. We didn't need to discuss the unknowns hanging over our relationship. The mornings were for us, our safe rhythm tucked away from the desires of the Fae.

When we were done, we parted ways in front of the Mother's house.

"Good luck," Daylen said. He kissed my forehead, his lips lingering over me.

I looked upward to kiss him back, but then Jaria opened the door. I dropped away from Daylen.

"Good. You're here," Jaria said. She didn't even look at Daylen. "I was about to go looking for you. You shouldn't be late for your first day."

"No, I guess not." I looked to the ground. I didn't mean to be rude, but I wished Jaria could've delayed a few seconds longer.

"I'll see you tonight?" Daylen asked.

"At the community house," I replied.

Jaria ignored us and began walking to the perimeter. After one final glance towards Daylen, I followed after her. My nervousness mixed with excitement. Who knew what experiences were possible on the first day of high school?

We stepped into the car together, and Jaria pointed out a backpack she had stored in the back seat. I opened it and checked its contents while we drove to school. The pack was loaded with strange things: pens, pencils, notebooks, and a device I realized was a calculator.

My stomach twisted as I looked at all of it. I knew how to write, vaguely, but had never tested myself. I didn't know much about math.

"Do the Fae really care that I do well in school?" I asked Jaria. "I'm Bigfoot, after all, none of this really matters, right? It's all a game."

Jaria clicked her tongue. "Yes, it matters."

"I somehow know things," I said. "Human things. Usually, it's words like *t-shirt* or *calculator*. Will I know human things, like history or math? Are you sure I can really pass as human? They've had years of education by now."

"You'll know some things," Jaria said. "That crystal of yours allows you to access the collective Fae knowledge. Part of my role is expanding that knowledge, but the Fae don't know everything. Your pendant will add any new information you learn to the collection. It should make school easier for you since you won't need to memorize information. If you learn something once, you'll know through the pendant."

She was right, this would help, but I thought about math or language arts. The moment a question took critical thinking, I'd be in trouble, even with the pendant's help.

I wiggled deeper into my seat. Playing volleyball was going to be much more fun than school.

The car pulled behind a long line of vehicles in front of the high school and began to crawl forward to the front of the building. Despite having visited every day for the last week, the school was practically unrecognizable. It'd been empty before, but now I felt like I was about to walk into a zoo.

Students crowded the pavement. Some of the girls wore beautiful clothes and faces caked with makeup. Others covered themselves in layers of clothing despite the warm temperature.

I pulled down the car mirror and evaluated my reflection. Human hair still didn't make any sense to me, and I'd never tried makeup. I looked at my clothes and realized how common they were. Another t-shirt and jeans. I looked like everyone else. Was it a good or bad thing?

"It doesn't matter," Jaria said. "You're not one of them anyhow."

She was right. I wasn't one of them. Regardless, I feared standing out and knew I'd be judged like I was human. I looked to my feet and felt like I was wearing clown shoes. I was still Bigfoot.

"Get on with it." Jaria must have reached for me. I felt her icy contact on my skin.

I pulled my arm back and stepped out of the car.

Without knowing where to go or who to talk to, I reverted to autopilot. I walked past the humans I didn't know.

I stepped out of the way when I saw girls squeal to embrace their friends. I looked away from the boys who compared who had grown the most muscle over the summer.

Lexi insisted on calling me an animal, but this human display was the most animalistic thing I'd ever seen.

I walked to the gym. It was the safest place I knew of. I was part of the team now, it wasn't only a familiar space, I belonged here.

The gym was more crowded than usual. Only one volleyball net was set up while the rest of the court was used for basketball.

I sighed with relief when I recognized the other girls playing at the volleyball net. It was the first time I was excited to see Lexi and Quinn. Olivia waved for me to join them, so I did.

I set my backpack in a pile with the others and stepped to the side of the court.

There were fifteen more minutes before I had to go to homeroom. I'd rather be here than there. Lexi might be a bully, but at least she wasn't a stranger.

The school seemed as big as my entire village. I couldn't understand the idea of this many humans together. And this was only one town. What about cities? Or the rest of the country? The world?

My brain shut down the thought before I could even try to comprehend the size of humanity.

My discomfort faded as I took my place on the court. The game was becoming familiar.

I waved when Payton arrived. We hadn't planned to meet here this morning, but maybe, just like me, this was where she wanted to be. She fell in with the other team, and we continued to play.

The game ended once a bell rang indicating there were only five more minutes before homeroom started. I still didn't know where to go.

I picked up my bag and dug through it, relieved to find the paper with my class schedule printed on it.

"Higgins?" I said, reading off my homeroom teacher. "Is that Coach Higgins?"

"Yep," Olivia answered. "She teaches social studies." Olivia pointed out of the gym, "Head out and take a left. Go up to the second floor, you'll find the room quickly enough." Olivia looked to Payton. "Where are you headed?"

"Bishops," Payton replied.

"Math teacher," Olivia said. "Leave the same way as Alice but go up to the third floor."

"Thanks," Payton said.

"If you want to be with the team over lunch, meet here." Olivia began walking to her own homeroom. "Join us."

I nodded because I was overwhelmed. Now that volleyball was over, my nervousness returned in full force. My heart raced in pace with a hallway full of students scrambling to get to class before the second bell rang.

"Let's go," Payton shouldered her bag and began walking where Olivia had pointed.

I followed after her as we navigated the crowded halls to the stairs. I stepped off on the second floor while Payton moved on to the third. I wished we had homeroom together.

I wanted her with me, even if it was only for a few more minutes.

I walked by the classrooms, located Coach Higgins' room, and stepped inside.

I stayed near the door, and frozen in place, scanned the room. Desks and chairs. It should be easy to pick one, but it wasn't. There were rules here that I didn't understand.

I reviewed my classmates from the door, scanning them. Many of them seemed to already know each other. I hoped there would be someone I recognized from volleyball camp, but there wasn't.

Then I smelled him.

A familiar human scent pulled me back to the forest, reminding me of the day I had first discovered my powers. I scanned the chairs and found the boy from the forest. Mark.

He waved when he saw me. I wanted to bolt. I'd been so confused when we had first met, and I was afraid he knew I didn't belong.

Then the bell rang. Coach Higgins looked up from her desk. "Alice, good to see you! Take a seat, and I'll get started with attendance."

There was an open desk next to Mark. I took it.

Chapter 21

Coach Higgins asked the students to quiet down. "Attendance first," she said and proceeded to read each of our names from a list. I followed everyone's example and said, 'here' when she called "Alice Turner."

I learned Mark's last name was Weston.

"Some announcements," Coach Higgins continued. "Most of you have been in my homeroom before." One of the boys sitting in the back snickered, he whispered some inside joke to the guy seated next to him. "As you know, I'm an easy-going teacher if you're easy-going students.

"I have three rules for homeroom: be present when class starts, be quiet during announcements and don't be rude to your classmates. We all share this homeroom together, there's no good reason to make it a bad experience for anybody else.

"So, let's get started on announcements." She pulled up a video on her computer and projected it to the class.

"Broadcast team strikes again," the boy in the back said.

"I'm pretty sure this is more entertaining than me reading announcements," Coach Higgins replied.

The boy didn't respond but allowed the video to play without further interruption.

Jack and Annie introduced themselves as our Monday broadcast team and invited Principal Evans onto the screen. The principal welcomed us to Piner High School and hoped we had all enjoyed our summers. Then they played a series of video clips summarizing some renovations that had been done to the school, volunteer work that had been done over the summer, and highlights from last years' graduating class.

I tried to blend in with my classmates and seem bored with the overly-animated video, but I couldn't help feeling amazed. How could there be this much change in one summer? I had grown up in a community that hadn't changed in living memory.

Bigfoot buildings were renovated but never changed. Houses were always passed down to the next family that needed them. How could humanity not only accomplish this much change but be able to respond to it?

"We hope you'll continue to grow with Piner High, shaping us for the future!" The video ended, and Jack and Annie signed off.

"You've got 5 minutes until the bell rings," Coach Higgins said, closing the video and ending the projection. "You can do what you want as long as it doesn't disturb your neighbors." She began to work on her laptop.

I pulled out my schedule and looked at the next period. I groaned.

"What's wrong?" Mark asked me.

"I've got math next," I replied.

"I assume you don't like math."

"I don't think I do." I couldn't confess to him that I really didn't understand much about math, one way or another. I knew enough to be intimidated.

"I'm not great at it," Mark said. "But I'm not lousy either. If you ever want to review your homework in homeroom, I'll help you."

It was kind of him to offer. Maybe I'd have to take him up on that at some point.

"If you're not great with math and your hunting is abysmal, what are you good at?" I didn't mean to be rude, but something in me wanted to push Mark and see how he'd react.

"I'm good at some things," he said, not giving a hint of embarrassment. "But it's all pretty useless."

"What are your strengths?" I asked.

"History, music, philosophy," He said.

"That's not useless! I sing like a screeching bat. What do you play?"

"A little guitar, a little ukulele."

"Ukulele?" I asked.

"Like they have in Hawaii. It's a little shrill. Maybe I'll play for you, and you can join as the screeching bat."

He was teasing me! I shoved him, a little, in play.

Mark pushed me away and smiled. He grabbed my schedule from my desk and began comparing it to his.

"We don't have any classes together," he observed.

"Bummer." I meant it. Mark was odd—no Bigfoot male would be casual about poor hunting skills—but he was interesting. He made me laugh.

"At least we'll have homeroom," he said. "We'll get to start every day together."

I blushed. Were we flirting? Did Mark think I liked him?

"Where are you from?" Mark asked. "I've never seen you before this summer."

"I was homeschooled," I said as Jaria had recommended. "My family doesn't get out very much."

"So, they sent you to high school?" He laughed.

"It hasn't been that bad so far! I made it onto the JV volleyball team!"

"You must be so proud of yourself."

"I am!" I said, then realized I sounded like a child seeking attention. "Are you in any clubs?"

"No," Mark considered, "but I hadn't thought about it either. Maybe I should do something. Dad says clubs are a waste of my time, but…you know perfectly well that my hunting is a waste of time too."

"Then why do you hunt?"

"Everyone else in my family does. It's important to Dad and my brothers that I can go hunting with them. I guess it's our family's thing."

"Your brothers?" I asked.

"Yeah, two of them. They're both older and more like the sons Dad wanted. Fortunately, it makes it easier for Dad to ignore me."

I was amazed to see how comfortably he talked about himself. It seemed impossible that this was the same boy who had seemed miserable in the forest.

"You like volleyball?" he asked me.

"I think I'll like it better than school," I said.

"School's not so bad. Do you like to know things?"

I nodded. I loved information but didn't recall it easily. Critical thinking was more Jaria's gift than mine.

"Then keep asking questions until you get your answers," he replied. "It's as simple as that."

"What about grades?" I asked.

"Irrelevant," Mark said. "Another way for people to compete. What matters is finding the answers you're looking for."

I nodded. I liked his answer better than any of the things Jaria had said about grades.

I met his eyes, they were blue. I'd never seen blue eyes so close before.

I wanted to tell him about me, but there was so much I couldn't say. How could I explain that every moment was an act, that I was always pretending to be someone I wasn't. I wasn't only ignorant as a freshman, but I was unaware as a human. How could someone like Mark ever understand my life?

There was something in his eyes, something familiar. He knew I was a fraud, but Mark had already accepted me.

I fought the impulse to tell him everything.

"It's hard, I know," Mark said. "We're all pretending to be someone tougher than we are. We pretend to be someone else. It's normal, it's human."

I looked away, unable to maintain our connection any longer. If I had fur, it'd be standing straight. Instead, I had goosebumps.

The bell rang. Relieved to get away, I turned away from him, grabbed my bag, and left the classroom.

I was already missing his straightforward speech by the time I stepped out the door and into the busy hallway.

Chapter 22

My first day of school was somehow both confusing and boring at the same time. Every time the bell rang, I'd go to a new class. There, teachers would distribute their syllabus and textbooks. Some teachers seemed just as disinterested in the subject as the students, but others demanded strict attention.

I met lots of other students. I tried to memorize their names and faces, but humans looked so similar to each other with their squishy faces. Soon, everyone blurred together, and I realized it'd take me a long time before I'd be able to identify my classmates.

Lunch was a disappointment. The food paled in comparison to what Tami had cooked for us. Even the frozen pizza had been better.

I grabbed a slice of pizza and took it to the gym. As Olivia had promised, the team was there. Some were casually throwing the ball around, while others sat and talked.

Payton wasn't anywhere in sight, maybe she had a different lunch period, so I sat down on the bleachers and began to eat alone.

Olivia and Lexi were talking nearby. I didn't mean to eavesdrop, but it was the most exciting thing around me.

"Are you applying anywhere else?" Lexi asked.

"Maybe," Olivia replied. "I could send my videos to more universities farther away. There are other schools I don't like as much that don't have my application…but does it matter how much I like the school? I just want someone to take me on their team."

"You really want to keep playing, don't you?" Lexi asked.

"Yes."

"I don't think I want to play in college," Lexi admitted.

"Really?" Olivia seemed shocked

"Yeah," Lexi began talking faster like she wasn't comfortable with the words coming from her own mouth. "I'm tired of it. Being good at a sport takes so much time. It's only going to get worse in college. I'm ready to do something else."

"Would you really quit? You're going to get a huge scholarship."

"I know—"

"But money isn't everything, is it?" Olivia admitted.

"The way Mom treats it," Lexi continued, "if I don't make a volleyball team, I might as well not go to college. But every time I think of committing to another four years of play, I feel sick inside. I can't do it."

"Have you told your mom?"

"No! Of course not. She'd go on and on about 'so many years of training wasted,'" Lexi said with a mocking voice.

Olivia giggled. "That sounds like her."

I finished my pizza and walked away to clean my hands before joining the others on the court.

I hated it, but by overhearing that conversation, I'd become sympathetic to Lexi. There was something in her tone that wasn't consistent with the bully I thought she was.

But then I recalled her voice in my mind, all the times she had called me an animal. No, I wouldn't feel pity for her.

The afternoon slid by. Sometimes it was fast and other times dreadfully slow.

Once the school day was over, I joined my team for practice. The training was much harder than any day at camp had been. I'd felt fresh each morning at camp, but today I was already tired from school.

Jaria picked me up from school after practice was done. While we rode, I allowed Jaria to barrage me with advice and comments. I was too tired to contribute or to tell her to back off.

"You'll have to do your homework," Jaria said as the car parked in the garage.

"I got most of it done in study hall," I said. "I'll finish the rest in the morning." Not only was school going to take up my entire day, but Jaria wanted it to consume my nights too?

"You should finish it tonight," Jaria said. "It's one of the main reasons I had the house built."

I opened the door and stepped into the living space. I dropped my schoolbag at the desk but didn't open it.

"Sure," I said, "if I'm going to learn to be both Bigfoot and human, it's obviously best for me to spend all my time in a human body. Shouldn't I spend more time with our people?" My voice was getting louder, my frustration was becoming harder to hide. I wanted to go home.

"This house has electricity and Internet," Jaria said. "Besides, you shouldn't bring your human textbooks into the village. It'll cause too many problems if anyone finds them."

I sighed. "This is really nice and everything, I appreciate the effort you put into building this beautiful house. But the truth is I want to go to my real home. I want to see my family and suitor."

Jaria didn't reply.

"These human days are so long," I continued, "and I'm not even sure who I am by the end of the day. Am I Alice the Bigfoot or am I Alice Turner?"

I waited for Jaria to respond. I stared at nothing, oriented towards where I had last heard her. Finally, she spoke, "I know. Sorry if I've put too much pressure on you."

"But," I began for her.

"But the Fae need this," Jaria said. "Our people need this. This isn't some game for the Fae, this is about the future of the Bigfoot people. It's my role to help you become the person the Fae need."

"And the Fae really need me to be a good student?"

"They hope you'll go to college one day."

"College?" I struggled to grasp the concept. "Like Olivia and Lexi?"

"The Fae believe it would help our cause if you had an advanced education."

"Then what happens? Even if I'm accepted into a university, they're all hours away from here. How can I become a college student and still be part of our community? Will I disappear from the village, like my ma did?"

"I thought you were okay with this," Jaria said.

I thought I'd been okay with this too. But the Fae kept asking for me to give up a little bit more.

First, they needed me to give up Daylen, and now they thought I should go to college. They wanted me to move away from the forest? If I did that, I'd be human all the time. Could I still be a genuine Bigfoot anymore?

"You don't have to make a decision yet," Jaria reminded me.

"Yeah," I said, sitting down in the desk chair. I was relieved to see a laptop and cell phone sitting there. "Thanks for the electronics," I said, pulling my books from my bag.

"You're welcome," Jaria said.

I ignored her and began reviewing my school work.

Chapter 23

After Monday, the week sped by. Thursday, and my first volleyball match, came before I was ready for it.

The team met after school, and instead of training in the gym, we packed our bags. Both the JV and varsity teams loaded onto a school bus parked outside of the high school.

My heart rate began accelerating as I stepped onto the school bus. It reminded me of the heroines I'd seen in Payton's movies who had sweaty palms before a battle. Maybe this was what Pa or Daylen experienced before a hunt. I was excited, I was nervous. I wanted to win and feared what I'd feel if we lost.

I sat with Payton, and we talked, nervously, about the strategy we had learned. I asked what she knew about Greenwood High School and discovered it was part of our school's conference and, like every school we competed against, more than an hour away.

"Are your parents coming?" Payton asked. "My mom can't make it. She tried to get tonight off, but it didn't work out."

"I'm sure she'll make it to another game," I said to be kind. Truthfully, I hadn't thought about parents coming to games.

"What about your parents?" Payton asked.

I smiled, amused by the idea of Stepma and Pa coming to a game. I didn't know which was funnier: the idea of Bigfoots sitting in bleachers with humans or trying to explain volleyball to my family. "I don't think they'll be making it to any games."

"Oh, I'm sorry." Payton seemed worried on my behalf as if she was ready to comfort me because of my absent parents.

I wished I could tell her that it was okay. My parents weren't worried about my grades or how my volleyball games went. They only cared about my safety.

Payton and I tried to do homework while on the bus. It was only week one, but the workload was beginning to pile up. I had a book to read, but I was slow at reading. There was a math assignment to complete, but I was missing years of introduction to the subject.

In the end, I skimmed the book and scribbled down awful answers to the math problems. Jaria wouldn't be too pleased, but the game was more important to me. One day of poor homework couldn't matter that much.

As we neared the school, Lexi and Olivia taught us our cheers. All the older students already knew them, and it was easy to learn.

Lumber Ladies strike them down,
Lumber Ladies hit them hard,
score the point, win the set
Lumber Ladies will win this match!

There was some confusion about whether the team should say "Lumber Ladies" instead of "Lumber Jacks," but Olivia ended it. "We're the Lumber Ladies. I don't care what the uniforms say. Would you rather be Lumber Jills?" Nobody wanted to be the Lumber Jills.

By the time we were done practicing, the bus was parked outside the school, and every member of our team was standing. The energy was contagious, and soon, the team was humming with anticipation.

Coach Nelson stood up and whistled for silence. The team quieted, but nobody sat back down.

"Alright ladies, we've got about 45 minutes before the JV match starts. The varsity match will be half an hour after JV is done. As soon as we're in the gym, get your uniforms on and start warming up."

Then she continued to announce the starters for both teams. My stomach clenched as I waited through the varsity names.

"For JV, we have Alice..."

My body trembled with anticipation. I'd get to play today. I was so happy, being stuck on the sidelines sounded awful.

Payton's name wasn't called, but she punched my arm to say, "Nice work."

"You'll get time," I said.

Payton shrugged. "At least I'm here."

Lexi and Olivia led the team from the bus. They walked confidently through the halls of the school, past the gym, and into the locker room. Payton and I followed after them, pretending we were as comfortable in this strange environment as they seemed to be.

Truthfully, my stomach was rolling inside me. This was the farthest from home I'd ever been. It was crazy to know this was only the beginning of the adventures that the Fae had in store for me.

I struggled to focus on the drills while we warmed up. I tried to remind myself that even though the gym looked different, the court remained the same. The volleyballs were identical to the ones I always played with. The net was at a height that I knew.

I was the farthest from my village that I'd ever traveled. The knowledge elevated my fear of exposure. I hadn't been this uncomfortable with humans since the first day.

While we had ridden to the school, I had tried to track the bus's route. I thought I knew how to get home on my own, but we had come a long way. Not that it should matter. I had my phone and trusted Jaria was looking out for me. There shouldn't be any trouble I couldn't get myself out of.

I didn't have time to worry about that now. All that mattered was that I was a starter for my team. My team needed me to be focused, and I couldn't help them if I was distracted.

Warm-up passed quickly, and before I was ready, Coach Higgins was giving a pregame speech. It started with a bit of strategy and ended with excitement. Lexi led the team through the cheer one more time.

By the time we were done, my arms, legs, and entire body were tingling with energy. I ran into position, bouncing on my feet.

Ellie walked to center court and told the referee we wanted heads. A girl on the other side of the net flipped the coin. It was heads.

The team clapped their hands as Ellie took the ball and jogged to the serving position.

The ref blew the whistle, and I held my breath as Ellie threw the ball into the air. Time seemed to slow as the ball drifted back towards her.

—smack—

Ellie struck the ball with her palm, and it soared into the sky, falling towards the players on the other side of the net.

One of the opponent girls returned the ball to the air and then a second hit the ball, setting up a play. A third player whacked the ball to our side of the net.

The ball was falling right in front of me, but despite all my energy, I suddenly felt frozen into place.

I should've responded already—it was going to be too late—the ball was about to hit the ground. If I didn't do something now, they'd score.

Then I stopped thinking.

My body moved of its own accord, dropping low, making up for a missed opportunity. I raised my arms just in time to return the ball back into the air.

I exhaled, sighing with relief that I hadn't missed the ball.

"Alice, don't over-analyze," Coach Higgins said from the sidelines.

I nodded in agreement. I watched while another teammate set the ball, launching it back my direction.

I jumped upward, extending my reach to its full advantage. I made contact with the ball and spiked it downward, smacking it on the other side of the net.

I moved too fast and powerfully. The girl on the other team couldn't reach the ball in time. It smacked against the floor with a satisfying clap.

I heard my team cheering from the sidelines but didn't look their way. I didn't want to listen to them. All I allowed myself to feel was the thrill of adrenaline as I lowered my weight, preparing to jump forward and strike the next ball that came my way.

After that first point, I found my rhythm. I slid into the game, losing context of the world beyond the court.

I played, rotating with my team and taking serves. I set up plays and struck them down. I praised my teammates whenever they scored.

I tried not to yell in disappointment when a teammate missed, and the ball fell to the floor. Despite my effort, I knew my reaction showed on my face.

"Alice the Animal." I heard someone say from the bleachers where the varsity girls sat. I turned, teeth gnashed, and was surprised to see it wasn't Lexi who had said it.

It was Olivia. She had called me 'Alice the Animal.'

But she was nodding her head, smiling with approval. This wasn't an insult, she meant it as a compliment.

Yet, the words stung. I was a Bigfoot. That meant I was close enough to an animal as far as humans would be concerned.

But I couldn't be angry with Olivia, she had seen something in me before anyone else did. Maybe I really was good at volleyball because I was, in some ways, an animal.

I didn't want to become Alice the Animal, but maybe I could be her for the sake of my team.

I stood straighter and wondered how Pa would feel about being called an animal. He'd be proud, focused, and ready to beat the competition.

We won the first set. Then the second, making us 2-0. If we won one more set, we would win the match.

Coach Higgins made me sit out the third set, and Payton was substituted into play along with most of the girls from the bench. I cheered loudly from the sideline, struggling to sit and rest my legs.

These girls were my team, and I wanted to help them succeed. Unfortunately, we lost the third set, and now the score was 2-1. We needed to win a third set to win the match. Now that I was rested, Coach Higgins sent me back in.

The last game flowed from me, time became irrelevant while I played. Soon, it was our match-point.

Ellie hit the ball over the net. I held my breath as I watched it near the ground and exhaled when the ball struck the floor. I raised my arms in celebration.

We had won the fourth set. It was 3-1.

That meant our team had won the match.

I cheered, adrenaline pumping through me as we walked to the net. I followed my teammates as we high-fived the team from Greenwood High School and told them 'good job.' I tried to be genuine, but I knew I wouldn't have felt so great if we hadn't won the match.

I stretched on the sidelines while the varsity team warmed up, struggling to work the adrenaline from my veins. Soon, I returned to the bleachers. While it was hard to hold still at first, the longer I rested, the more tired I became. Soon, I'd eaten all the snacks I had taken from my human home. I vowed to pack more food next time.

"Really owning your nickname?" Lexi said, hovering nearby and holding a volleyball against her hip. "Animals need lots of food, right?"

Part of me wanted to hit her, but I knew Coach Nelson would never stand for it. No, our fight was limited to a nickname I pretended to be comfortable with. I waved my hand dismissively and Lexi returned to the court.

I watched the varsity girls play, quietly talking it over with Payton. We commented on our teammates as we watched them, learning how they played the game.

I wished Lexi wasn't so good. I was tired of watching her, but it was hard to look away.

Lexi seemed to know the future. She knew where the ball was going to be and how to be in the right place before she was needed. She moved with grace, and whenever she hit the ball, it landed exactly where she wanted it.

I wished I could play like her. I was a natural and getting better, but Lexi's skill left me in the dust.

As I watched, I began to notice a woman in the stands. She sat alone and muttered under her breath. She squeezed a stress ball in one hand and yelled whenever Lexi touched the ball.

"That's Lexi's mom," Payton told me.

When Lexi inevitably did miss, the woman yelled. Actually animalistic. The sound was terrible. Lexi had to have heard it but didn't look up. She didn't acknowledge her mother in the stands.

I wanted to feel sorry for Lexi, but I couldn't. At least she had a ma, she didn't know how thankful she should be that her parents were even at the game.

I knew that wasn't fair of me. But Lexi wasn't reasonable to me either. She didn't deserve my pity.

The fifth set ended with a third victory for the Lumber Ladies. The varsity match had run longer than the JV's, and by the time they were saying 'good job,' I was almost asleep in the bleachers.

We gathered around Coach Nelson, who gave a few more final words. She congratulated us on our wins and told us she'd review the game in detail at tomorrow's practice. Lexi led us through one last cheer, but it wasn't as loud as the first had been. Everyone was exhausted.

Most of the girls left with their parents, but I rode the bus back home with Payton. Jaria called my phone and offered to pick me up, but I told her I was okay. I didn't tell her I'd rather share the hour ride with Payton than listen to Jaria's examination of my play.

The bus ride home was quiet, we sat on benches across from each other and then laid out. I tried to do more homework, but gave up and began to doze instead.

When we reached the parking lot, I saw the Fae car was already waiting for me. I waved goodbye to Payton as she began walking home.

Jaria talked too much as we drove back to the house. She asked about my homework, and I told her I did it all on the bus, avoiding the fact that a few of my answers were nonsense. She continued talking about my volleyball play as we walked back to the village together.

I stopped by the community house on my way back home and pulled Daylen to a corner table. While resting my head against the table's surface, I told him all about my day.

He listened, enthralled, as I tried to explain what it was like to be part of a team. I told him about the adrenaline.

"You sound like a hunter," he said with awe.

I considered what I'd experienced in Piner. I compared how Pa talked about hunting to the woman I had watched in Payton's movies.

I met his gaze. "The humans allow their females to be like hunters. I've seen it in movies."

I expected him to frown in disgust. I should've been judging the human way, not admiring it.

Instead, Daylen smiled.

"You would make a good hunter." He said without judgment.

Over dinner, I wondered what Pa would think of the sport I was playing. Would he be proud of me? Or would he be frustrated that I wasn't growing into a regular Bigfoot?

As I fell asleep, I allowed myself to consider if Ma would have been proud. I figured she would be.

Chapter 24

The next morning in homeroom, the official announcements said nothing about the volleyball team's victory. Instead, Coach Higgins spoke after turning off the screen, "As coach of the volleyball team, I want to add that both our varsity and JV teams won their matches against Greenwood High School last night."

There was light applause.

"And congratulations to our very own Alice Turner," she motioned to me. I blushed, wishing she wouldn't point me out. "The JV's victory would've been much more difficult without her."

The room clapped a little louder. I sat taller because I thought I should and smiled nice because that seemed right too. But inside, I wanted to hide. The fewer people who saw me, the less likely anyone would realize that I didn't belong.

I lifted my gaze and dared to look at Mark, sitting at the desk next to mine. He was clapping louder than everyone else combined and grinning like he had been given a truck full of ice cream.

I shoved him playfully. "Stop that."

He stopped clapping but kept smiling. My heart pounded while I considered his face. This was a good look for him. He had to be the most attractive human boy I'd met.

Best of all, he seemed to understand what it meant to be human in a way that I couldn't comprehend. It was in the little things he said: the snide comments he made or the way he questioned perspectives everyone else took to be fact.

Jaria reminded me to fit in, but Mark pushed himself against the grain, fighting to be unique. Watching him inspired me to do the same.

I was beginning to wonder if there were two ways before me. There was the good Alice, the student-athlete who did whatever the Fae asked.

But there was something else, too. Someone else that I could become. I could make my own path here, pushing the limits of the Fae and testing what the boundaries of humanity were.

And Mark saw that, in his way. He knew I was acting, just like he knew everybody was.

My relationship with Mark was different than with Payton. Payton didn't doubt me but trusted me unconditionally. The knowledge that I was lying to her with my very appearance made my insides twist. Payton was honest and didn't expect me to be lying to her.

But Mark accepted my deception. He knew everyone was in disguise.

Mark could see through the distractions and the noise, he had found the heart of the matter. He understood something important about what it really meant to be human, and I wanted him to teach me.

As I studied his smile. I wondered what it'd be like to do more than push him in play. Would it really be that bad to let my fleshy skin touch that of another human—

I ended the thought before it could go any further.

Instead, I thought of Daylen, imagining his warmth and affection. Daylen saw me clearly too, in a way Mark never could. Mark was only human, but Daylen was one of my own.

Searching for a distraction, I pulled out my math homework. I considered the last few problems and groaned. My answers were utterly useless. I began to erase the final solution.

Mark looked over my work as I tediously restarted the problem. He didn't know the solutions, but he did offer his ideas. By the time we were packing our bags, we had redone the last three problems.

I couldn't afford to be attracted to Mark, but maybe, he could still be my friend.

"Alice, can I have a word?" Coach Higgins called from her desk. The bell was about to ring.

I walked over. "How can I help you?"

She studied me, taking the time to choose her words. "Alice, you've got talent. And it isn't just your height. You're fast and have good instincts. I know you're new to volleyball, but you've learned fast."

"Thank you," I said, unsure where this was going.

"I wanted to tell you to keep it up. The season is short, but it's intense. I know you'll get busy and tired before it's over."

I nodded. It was true. I was wondering how I was going to keep up with my school work and play weekly volleyball matches. It was only the first week, and I was already exhausted.

Coach Higgins continued, "With some practice, you'll probably make varsity next year."

"Thank you," I said, but I didn't dare to feel like Coach Higgins saw something in me. She probably said this to everyone.

Everything would be easier if nobody expected anything from me. But that wasn't this path. Jaria, on behalf of the Fae, needed me to become a great student and athlete. Stepma and Pa wanted me to become an adult inside the village.

The real question was: what did I want? I had both a million answers and none at the same time.

Fortunately, the bell rang. It was time for math, and I didn't have time to answer uncomfortable questions.

Chapter 25

If the first week of school had gone by fast, it was nothing compared to how the semester passed. I had now entered the high-speed world of humans.

Between schoolwork, practices, and games, the days blurred together into an exhausting repetition. The weeks began adding up.

I loved every moment of it.

I was too busy to consider what could happen after the volleyball season was over, the semester ended, and the Winter Solstice arrived. I welcomed the distraction.

My relationship with Daylen continued to grow. Maybe he was my first suitor, and I was a lovesick adolescent, but I was wondering if we shared something special. Most suitors spent time together out of necessity, not always enjoying each other's company.

Our relationship was different. Trapping with him every day was worth the early mornings. Our conversations flowed with ease and silences were comfortable.

Occasionally, we would sneak away. Then, hidden among the trees, we could kiss. Kissing Daylen was the discovery of a whole new world of physical affection. My body longed for Daylen in ways that I'd never known possible.

I was beginning to wonder if I loved Daylen. I considered telling him, but I wasn't sure. Somedays, I didn't recognize myself, so how could I know who I loved? The last thing I wanted to do was hurt him if I was wrong.

The more my relationship with Daylen deepened, the guiltier I felt about Mark. I omitted Mark from my conversations with Daylen. It hadn't been intentional, but after a while, I felt strange bringing him up after avoiding the subject for so long.

How could I even explain Mark to Daylen? They were opposites. While Daylen strived to be a good, strong, male within the village, Mark seemed just as confident standing in opposition to expectations.

So, while my feelings for Daylen deepened, my affection for Mark developed. Mark said what everyone else wouldn't admit. I could listen to his thoughts every day in homeroom without tiring.

I convinced myself that my interest in him was that of a friend, of a non-human searching for understanding. But, thanks to Mark, homeroom became my favorite part of the school day.

I grew tired of pretending to like Daylen's friends at the community house in the evening and began visiting Payton's home to hang out with her instead.

When she was home, Tami cooked the best food with the most delicious smells while we did our homework at the table. We ate the fantastic food together before ending our evening with a TV show or part of a movie.

If Payton found it strange that I didn't go into town on the weekends or that she never met my family, she didn't comment on it. This privacy was the most amazing gift from a friend.

I loved Payton for being so accepting, but it was uncomfortable to know I was betraying her with my very appearance. The problem had no easy solution, and my guilt became a familiar companion.

At night, I began to dream as Alice Turner. I dreamed of the volleyball court or the classroom. In those dreams, I was human. Slowly, my human body was starting to feel more real than my actual appearance.

Soon, it was fall. The mornings were colder, and the light was growing shorter. The rain was coming more frequently. It tried to snow, but it didn't stick to the ground.

And as winter approached, so did the volleyball championships.

I had played the entire season as a prominent member of the JV team. It'd been an unexpected blessing. My position had given me more experience than I could've had as a secondary member on the varsity team.

And so, after securing a win for the final JV match, Coach Higgins approached me and asked if I'd train with the varsity team until their season was over. Of course, I said yes.

The varsity team had a strong season with six wins out of eight games. It was a good record, and the team was invited to play in the single-elimination championship bracket.

Over the season, Quinn had suffered a knee injury. It wasn't so bad that she couldn't play, but she needed rest. She insisted on practicing, but her lousy knee slowed her down and limited her jumps. It had only gotten worse as the season progressed.

Coach Nelson had been vague about why I was training with varsity, but I understood what was at stake.

If Quinn couldn't play, I'd be shifted onto the varsity team for the championship games.

Lexi worked desperately with Quinn, trying to help her recover. They could almost be sisters. Quinn looked up to Lexi and Lexi wanted Quinn to be able to play.

But, in the end, Lexi's help came to nothing. The championship game was soon, but Quinn wasn't recovered.

Even though I'd been practicing with the varsity girls for only a week, my approach to the game had blended seamlessly with the team, as if I'd been working with them all season.

Nobody was surprised when, the day before the championship weekend, Coach Nelson called the team into a huddle. She announced that I'd be part of the varsity team, then she pulled Quinn aside to remind her she could still travel with the team to the game and that there would always be next season.

Jaria was late picking me up from school that day, and I waited near the pickup lane. The waiting made me irritable. I simultaneously wanted to brag to Jaria that I had made the varsity team and avoid any extra expectations from Jaria. As usual, my desires were contradictory.

It was a cool autumn day, and I had finally surrendered to the chilly temperatures and worn a sweater. It was fuzzy and reminded me how it would feel to be in my Bigfoot fur.

"Alice?"

I turned to see Mark standing behind me. My heart fluttered in my chest. I usually only saw him in homeroom and wasn't prepared for the encounter.

I cleared my throat and ran my hands through my hair. I had just stepped out from volleyball practice and hoped he didn't think I looked or smelled gross.

"What are you doing here?" I asked.

He shrugged, casual as always. "I took your advice and joined a club."

"Which one?"

He looked away.

I shoved his arm in play, "Come on! I'll tell you something if you tell me which club you're in."

He laughed. "Tell me your thing first."

"I'll get to play with the varsity team for the championship match." It was the first time I allowed myself to feel excited that Quinn's injury had given me an opportunity.

"That's amazing! When do you—"

"Which club did you join?" I interrupted.

"Debate," he said to the ground.

"That's so cool!"

"My family won't think that. Told them I was working on my layup after school. But I'm pretty sure they knew that's a lie. I can't hide forever."

I nodded. I understood how it felt to want something different from your family. "Does it make you happy?" I asked.

He smiled, and his face brightened. I knew he was enjoying the club.

A horn honked from the loading zone, and I turned to see Jaria's car waiting for me.

"That's me," I said.

"I'll see you tomorrow?" he asked.

With the volleyball games, I wouldn't be in school tomorrow. "Maybe after the tournament," I replied.

"Can't wait to hear how you do, Miss Varsity."

There was something in his tone that made me blush.

I stepped into the car and immediately began babbling to Jaria about the switch in the varsity lineup. It was the best ploy I could think of to distract her from the fact that my gaze never left Mark as we drove away.

Chapter 26

Payton and I sat together on the bus ride to Orchard Grove High School where the championship games would be played. The entire JV team had been invited to watch the varsity team play. So, of course, Payton decided to come along.

We had planned to travel to the games before we had known I'd be playing. Neither of us would turn down the opportunity to skip a Friday from school and watch a volleyball championship instead.

Back when we had decided to watch the game, I'd planned to be sitting with my friends. I expected to be disappointed that my season was over, but free to relax.

Instead, my stomach was heavy with nerves. Not only was this my first varsity game, but this was a game that mattered. This was a single-elimination tournament. If we lost a match, we were done.

There wasn't any room for mistakes.

Payton tried to chat, but all my responses were short. I couldn't find any solace in small talk.

Then Payton began to babble. At first, she told me stories that were from movies or TV shows I hadn't seen. Once she ran out of material, she made up her own narratives. I liked her stories because the heroine always won.

I had mythical powers from the Fae, but the worry clenching in my stomach reminded me those were only stories. Real life was much more complicated than make-believe.

The more she comforted me, the guiltier I felt. I didn't deserve this good of a friend.

"I need to go talk with Olivia," I interrupted. "Just realized I have a question about quick sets."

"Sure," Payton scooted aside, and I rose from our bench.

I walked down the bus aisle a few rows. Olivia had a bench to herself across from the one Lexi and Quinn shared.

I fell into the seat beside Olivia.

"Hey, Olivia," I began, and she turned to look at me. "Um, sorry to bother you, but I had a quick question about doing a quick set—"

Quinn snorted.

I turned from Olivia to look her way. Quinn rolled her eyes.

"Course you have questions," Quinn said. "I'm the one who has been training with this team all season."

I glared at her, but Lexi set her hand on Quinn's leg and said, "Don't worry. Alice hasn't been wasting her time. She spent the whole season learning to overcome her animal instincts…"

I knew Lexi was trying to make me angry, but that didn't stop it from working.

Over the season, Lexi and I'd reached an unspoken truce, a way to coexist on a team without being friends. However, I'd accidentally broken that agreement when I'd taken Quinn's place on the varsity team.

I grabbed Lexi's wrist. It was easy to encircle it in my oversized hands. There were so many ways I wanted to tell her how I hated being called an animal.

"Stop it," Olivia said, pulling me away from Lexi. "We're a team, act like one."

"Only because you have an investment in the outcome," Lexi said.

"So do you. You want to win, don't you?" Olivia replied.

"Course I do, but you're the one who invited a college coach to watch."

Olivia bit her lip.

"There's going to be a coach?" I asked. "Watching you?"

Olivia nodded.

"Watching everyone," Lexi corrected. "There are good players on the other teams too."

"Anyhow," Olivia said, turning towards me. "What's your question?"

I asked it, and she responded kindly enough, but once she was done, Olivia turned back to the window. Her confidence was fading.

"You'll do great," I said, as I got up from the seat.

"Thanks," she seemed unconvinced. I wished I could tell her more, help her to relax, but no words seemed right.

I returned to sit next to Payton, and soon, the bus arrived at Orchard Grove High School. I tried not to gawk while we walked into the building and towards the gym, but I couldn't help myself.

We had traveled to plenty of high schools over the season, but our match against Orchard Grove had been a home game.

I remembered that match vividly. It was the first one that we lost. I'd been devastated for days afterward, continually wondering what I could've done better.

The girls on the Orchard Grove team had been perfect. Not only had they played a good game, but they wore coordinating ribbons in their hair to match their new uniforms. Their makeup had withstood their sweat. Even their gym bags had been matching.

Orchard Grove was clearly the top team in our conference. Everyone expected they'd win the tournament. My team was just thankful we didn't have to play them in the first round.

Instead, we would play Evergarden. We had already beaten them that season 3-1 and didn't question if we could do it again. Everyone assumed we would make it to the next round of the tournament.

Payton, Quinn, Ellie, and the other JV girls climbed into the bleachers. A part of me envied them. I was excited to play, but watching from the sidelines would've been far less stressful.

I followed the varsity girls as we set our bags in a pile. Together, we warmed up and began our drills. The routine was comforting. Maybe I was playing with a different team, but this was how I'd prepared for all my matches.

The gym was noisy, more so than a regular game. The bleachers were filled, not only by our JV team and the parents of my teammates but the seven other schools playing that day.

As I'd been practicing all season, I zoned in on my teammates and the ball. I ignored the distractions of my own insecurities.

When we finished warm-ups, Coach Nelson pulled the team into a huddle to review our strategy. Once she was done, she listed the starting lineup.

It included me.

Coach Nelson looked directly at me when she said: "I'm putting some of you outside your comfort zone, but that's because I want to see what you can do."

I nodded with the other girls.

Then Lexi brought the team inward and began leading our cheer. I prayed it wouldn't be the last time that season I got to say the words. I couldn't imagine waiting another nine months to be able to play again.

I took my place on the court, and Olivia stepped towards the ref. She called tails, but the coin was heads. Their serve.

We waited for the ref to blow the whistle. The game was about to begin.

Chapter 27

A shrill whistle sounded, signaling the start of the game. The Evergarden team served.

The ball was headed towards my side, between Olivia and me.

"Mine!" I called, jumping into position.

"Mine!" Olivia called a moment later.

I tried to stop my movement, but Olivia was already standing where I was landing. I attempted to step aside—but too late—we were tripping over each other when the ball fell to the ground.

We had failed to return it. Their point.

Olivia glared at me, reached to pick up the ball, and lofted it back over the net towards the Evergarden server.

"I said it was mine," I tried to say, but the words were barely audible.

"Focus." Olivia didn't look at me but stared at the Evergarden server. She bounced on her knees, preparing to leap wherever the ball landed next.

I'd been watching Olivia play all season. This wasn't like her. She was a great communicator and trusted her teammates to return the ball. Something about that college coach being there had changed her play, making her more aggressive.

As the game continued, I adjusted my play to better balance Olivia. She was more forward than usual, desperate for any contact with the ball. I gave her the space she needed but prepared to step in if she made a mistake.

It was close, but we won the first set. We were 1-0. I was exhausted by the end, but it was worth it. I had contributed to the team, and we had our first victory.

Coach Nelson asked me to sit out for the second match, saying, "You played well, but it's a long day. Get some rest." Then she substituted in a more experienced player.

I watched from the bench as Olivia grew more frustrated with each volley. The angrier she got, the worse she played.

Our team lost the second set. Now we were 1-1.

The team huddled around Coach Nelson, but she pulled Olivia aside. The two of them talked. When Coach Nelson returned, she didn't change the lineup for the third set.

I watched the third set from the sideline.

Olivia's play got worse with each mistake. She was more aggressive with every volley. I wanted her to succeed, and it hurt to watch her deteriorate.

Then, it was Evergarden's set-point. Olivia overshot her return. The ball flew to the other side of the net and landed out of bounds.

The sound of the ball striking the floor resonated through my being. We had lost the set.

Now our team was losing, 1-2. If we lost a third set, then we would lose the match. If we lost the match, we would be out of the tournament. Our season would be over.

My team had been confident before today, but now we were only a few mistakes from losing.

Once again, Coach Nelson pulled Olivia to the sidelines between the sets. But this time, when they returned, I could see the glassy look of Olivia's tearful eyes.

"Olivia needs to sit out for a while," Coach Nelson said, then she pointed at me. "Alice will play this set."

The team was silent. Even if Olivia was off her game, she was one of the best players on the team. By contrast, I was an unknown.

"I know Alice is new to this team," Coach Nelson continued, "but she's rested and has a knack for the sport. Keep it together, ladies. We can still win."

Olivia tried to lead the team through a quick cheer, but her voice caught with emotion. She struggled to form the words.

Instead, Lexi spoke up. "Come on, Olivia might be out, but we've got this. 'Go Team!' on the count of three."

We yelled, 'Go Team!' Maybe it was the noisy gym, but the cheer didn't sound as loud as usual.

Our team began to pull together. Our next few plays were solid, and we used that momentum to return into the flow of success. Soon, we were ahead. I began to hope that we could win the match. We just had to win this set. Then we had to win the one after that. Difficult, but not impossible.

Lexi threw me a perfect pass, and I jumped up, reaching over the net and spiking the ball downward. The opponent failed to return it. A kill.

Now that I was back in play, the opposing team didn't know how to handle me. I was tall and could jump high. I blocked balls they hoped my team would miss. I could reach over the net to spike balls to the ground.

As much as I hated Lexi, we played well together.

Our team won the fourth set. Now the match was 2-2, and we would play a tie-breaking 15-point set. The gymnasium roared with cheers as we won, not because they were necessarily excited to see us win, but that a fifth set was always exciting to watch.

We rested from the sidelines. Coach Nelson made her announcements. She was putting Olivia back into the game, and I'd continue to play.

I sat on the bench, relieved to be off my feet for a few minutes. I breathed.

Lexi sat down next to me, "Good set."

I didn't immediately realize that she was complimenting me.

"I mean it," she continued. "You've got skills, but don't mess this up for us. Olivia needs to impress that coach, and I need to win this game."

"I didn't know you cared," I said. It was a well-known fact that Lexi's mom cared more about her performance than Lexi did.

Lexi exhaled, acknowledging the sore spot, but said, "I do like to win."

She stood up and returned to sit with her friends. I looked back towards Payton, sitting a few rows behind me. She was tense with excitement. "You're doing great!" she yelled. I waved back at her.

A woman stepped from the bleachers and began to talk with Coach Nelson. It was Lexi's mom, easily identifiable from all the matches I'd seen her attend. I watched her talk briefly with Coach Nelson and then to her daughter. I tried not to hear their conversation, but I heard enough to know that Lexi wasn't playing up to her mother's standards.

Coach Nelson told Lexi's mom to return to her seat, but Lexi's mom added one more sharp remark before sitting down. Coach Nelson apologized to Lexi, but Lexi shrugged and said, "I hear that all the time."

The ref blew the whistle. It was time to return to the court and begin the final set.

The set was tight. The crowd was tense with anticipation. Both teams were playing to their best ability, even with their players exhausted.

Whenever our team found the momentum to get ahead, we would lose it before sealing a victory. Then, the Evergarden girls would capture the energy for themselves. Not only was the volleyball vaulting between sides, but the strength of our teams was too.

Soon it was 14-14. If we could score two more consecutive points, we would win.

Lexi signaled that the next play was for Olivia, but Olivia froze up. She missed. It was 14-15. Their match point.

Lexi yelled to our girls, signaling that I should prepare for a quick set. We had to score, we had to get the serve back if we wanted to win.

This was the play I'd asked Olivia about on the bus. The timing of this was tricky, but Lexi was telling me to take it. She trusted me to finish this play.

Lexi passed the ball upwards, spinning it for the strike. She was giving me another perfect pass.

I leapt but moved too slowly. The ball rolled off my fingertips, falling weakly to the other side of the net.

Evergarden blocked the play.

I tried to take my mistake in stride but could feel Lexi's disappointment radiating like a source of heat.

It was a good play, one that she and Quinn had perfected. Lexi had done her part to give me a great pass. I was the one who had failed to deliver.

But Lexi had moved on, shouting to defend Evergreen's next play.

I helped with a block, but Lexi passed it back to Olivia to try and score.

Evergarden returned it, smacking it towards our side of the court.

"Mine!" Lexi shouted, leaping to the ground for a dig.

She missed.

The ball struck the ground, not her arms.

I heard the cheer before I understood what it meant. Evergarden had won their match point. We had lost 14-16.

We were out of the tournament. The season was over.

Chapter 28

For the first time all season, I took my time in the locker room.

The next match of the tournament had started. I heard the squeaking of sneakers and a crowd cheering. I'd already changed into my clean clothes, and there was no reason to be in the locker room.

Yet, I lingered.

I couldn't believe the season was over. Now, I'd spend the next nine months remembering how I'd failed the last time I had played in a game.

Most of the team had already left with their parents, but the bus wouldn't go until the last game of the day was over. Coach Nelson had said something about being supportive to the other girls in our conference. She had also mentioned we should watch the girls from Orchard Grove play.

Once, the idea of watching tournament play had excited me. But I wasn't in the mood anymore.

Instead, sitting on a cold locker room bench was better than being in the bleachers.

I shifted the crystal pendant between my hands. I hardly thought about it anymore. It had become another part of me, an accessory to my identity. Right now, it was a good distraction. I observed the different colors that came and went while I rotated it in the light.

I knew I should've been proud of my season. After all, I hadn't even heard of volleyball until the first day of camp. Regardless, I progressed to become a critical JV player and then stepped in for the varsity's championship match.

Yet…

The loss weighed me down. It was like my insides were nailed to the bench, pulling me down and keeping me inside the locker room.

I replayed my final moment of failure. I reviewed how the ball had slipped on my fingertips. If only I hadn't taken that extra moment to react. If I'd known the play better, maybe we could've scored.

If I'd scored, Evergreen wouldn't have reached match point. Then we could've served. The momentum could've shifted to our side of the court.

Maybe we could have won…if I hadn't made that mistake.

"She's in here," I heard someone say from the locker room door. I recognized her overly perfumed scent. Lexi.

She stepped into the locker room, Ellie and Quinn following behind her.

Lexi scanned me and scowled. "No wonder it smells like animal." She waved her hand in front of her nose to make her point. "If you're not going to watch the tournament, then at least take a shower.

She wanted to talk more about me and not showering. I wasn't interested. I looked away from them and back down at the crystal.

"Alice the Animal," Quinn said, nodding her head along to Lexi's words. Ellie nodded too.

Lexi walked closer, reaching the bench where I sat. Quinn stood behind her. Ellie moved behind me. There was only the four of us in the locker room.

"My mom's mad at me," Lexi said. "She drove off after the game. Didn't even want to speak to me."

"I'm…sorry?" I replied.

"You should be," Lexi continued. "I sent you a perfect pass, why didn't you complete the play?"

"I—the ball rolled off my fingertips—" I tried to say.

"I could have done it," Quinn said. "Too bad I wasn't on the team today."

"It's a new play—" I said.

Lexi leaned over me. "That's not an excuse."

"No," Quinn repeated.

"If I've got to wait for the bus because I made a mistake," Lexi said, "why would you get to make excuses for yours?"

Lexi's face was now inches from mine. I wondered if I should spit at her, but that was too animalistic. This wasn't my village, I was pretending to be human. I clenched my fist, digging my nails into my palm. It was better than hitting her.

"Alice the Animal," Lexi continued. "You're taller than all of us. No room for mistakes."

I stood up. If Lexi wanted to make fun of my height, it was time to remind her how tall I was.

As I stood, my calves pushed against the bench behind me, I tried to step forward, but Lexi was blocking me.

Lexi saw I was off balance but didn't step aside.

Instead, Lexi pushed me.

I couldn't take a step back—not with the bench behind me—I fell. My butt hit the ceramic tile while my feet hung over the bench.

I tried to scramble back to my feet, but Quinn and Ellie had already grabbed my shoulders. They began pulling me to the showers.

"The Animal needs to be cleaned," Lexi said. She pushed me back to the ground every time I tried to get back up. I was tall and strong, but there were three of them, and I was already on the ground.

I roared with frustration as they pulled me into a shower stall.

"I wonder if she bites." Lexi reached forward to turn on the water.

Ellie and Quinn stood next to her, blocking my exit. Lexi stayed beyond the water's reach, but close enough to push me down if I dared to stand.

The fluid pounded against my back. This forceful water was nothing like bathing in the river. This was cold and unnatural, like rain made too heavy. I howled.

I craved for my own body. I wanted my claws. This dainty human form felt so pathetic compared to what I could be. If only…

I considered taking my pendant off. That'd scare them. Then I could prove to Lexi that I wasn't someone she could mess with.

But that'd mean breaking the one rule that I'd been taught my whole life: never expose myself to humans.

I wouldn't take off the pendant. Even if it'd save me from this humiliation.

I tried to stand another time. If I couldn't transform, I would have to win this battle as a human. Lexi couldn't hold me down forever.

I shifted to my feet, pushing up with as much momentum as possible. I'd fall on them if I had to.

Lexi pushed back against my body, but my direction could not be changed.

I leaned forward to step from the shower, but my sneakers slipped against the wet tiles.

I lost control and fell back to the ground. My face banged against the wall. Pain shot through my nose.

I tried to cry out, but the sound was garbled. My nostrils pooled with liquid, and I touched my nose. It stung but wasn't broken. Time held still as I watched the water pouring from my face and realized it was tainted with my blood.

Lexi froze. I could almost watch the thoughts on her face: this had gone further than she had meant this to go.

She knew she should stop, but it was thrilling to see me bleeding on the ground. She had power, and it was intoxicating.

Lexi lifted her leg, preparing to kick me.

"What's going on in here?" Someone asked from outside the showers.

I felt hope again. Someone was entering the locker room, and Lexi was about to be caught. Coach Nelson couldn't let her get away with this.

I rubbed the water from my eyes and looked closer. Olivia was here. Payton stood behind her.

Payton surged towards me, but Quinn blocked her.

Olivia scanned the scene, then looked to Lexi, "What are you doing?"

"What does it look like?" Lexi replied. "I'm helping Alice bathe. As you can see, she isn't very good at it."

"Why does she have a bloody nose?" Olivia asked.

"Alice…" Lexi said. "She resisted our help."

Olivia frowned.

"We would've won the game if Quinn had been playing," Lexi said. "If our team had been complete, you would've played your best game. That college coach would've given you a spot on their team."

Olivia wrapped her arms around herself like she wanted to disappear inside her own embrace.

"Alice is the reason you lost," Lexi continued.

Olivia's frowned deepened.

"You're not going to let her do this!" I shouted.

But Olivia turned around. She walked out the door.

For the first time since this beating had started, I wanted to cry. I thought Olivia cared about me, but she wouldn't stand up for me when I needed her most.

Payton tried to push past Quinn but didn't succeed.

Lexi bent down to look at me. She pulled the pendant from my chest and used it to yank my face closer to hers.

"The soap is over there," she said. "Don't forget to use it."

I nodded. Ever since I had banged my nose, my head had begun to ache, and my thoughts slowed.

It was a terrible truth, but I knew I was done. Without showing my true form, I couldn't fight my way out. I was going to have to do what I was told.

"This is pretty," Lexi said, pulling my pendant towards her face. "I'm going to take it."

I struggled under the pressure of the cord against the back of my neck. I reached for the pendant, desperate to keep it against my body.

The cord broke. Lexi lifted the crystal from my chest, victorious.

As the stone left me, I felt the familiar wave of heat, I saw the light flash.

There was the sensation of water pounding against my fur. The shower was just as ghastly as it had been against my skin.

My vision hazed with red.

Lexi had no idea what she had released. The last part of me that was pretending to be human was finally free.

I was Bigfoot, and nobody could hurt me without paying for it.

I growled again, but this time it sounded like it should. I gnashed my teeth and leapt towards Lexi.

Her eyes grew big, and she stopped moving, stunned.

I lifted my hand and prepared to strike her face with my claws. If she didn't move, it would only scar.

I began to land the strike—but before I could touch her flesh—something stopped me.

Someone had grabbed my arm, holding me back. Rage beat through my body, and I prepared to roar at whoever dared stop me now.

Only, it was another Bigfoot holding me back. Jaria had become visible.

Chapter 29

Jaria had stopped me from hitting Lexi. She took my pendant from Lexi's loose grip and handed it back to me. "Don't you dare lose that again," she said.

I played with the cord in my wet, bloody hands, trying to knot it.

"Can't you do that quicker?" Jaria complained.

My fingers were shaking too hard. I stopped trying.

"You've been here this whole time?" I shouted. "Why didn't you do anything? Is watching Lexi push me into a shower part of your human studies?"

Jaria took the cord from me, knotted it, and handed it back.

"Why didn't you do anything?" I repeated. "I know you're not my friend, but aren't you my ally?"

Jaria sighed, clearly displeased. "Can't we talk about this later?"

I looked from Lexi to Quinn and Ellie. Finally, I looked at Payton. Her eyes were bright, torn between fear and amazement. As much as I hated it, Jaria was right, and I could fight with her later.

"I can handle these three," Jaria said, lifting her pendant before Lexi, Quinn, and Ellie. "I'll let you take care of that one. She's your friend, after all."

She meant Payton.

"What do you want me to do?" I asked.

"A little memory work." Jaria made it sound obvious, but I had no idea what she wanted from me. "Quickly, we need to do this before the memory has time to set."

Jaria lifted her pendant up. Quinn, Lexi, and Ellie seemed transfixed by it. She allowed it to start swinging. First left, then right.

"I can't do that!" I protested. "Not to Payton!"

"Either you do it," Jaria said, "or I'll do it for you."

I held the corded pendant in my hand and rose it to Payton's eye level. She looked at it the same way the others had. Her eyes began to glaze over.

"Alice?" Payton asked. "Is that really you? What's going on?"

"Quickly," Jaria said. "Who knows when someone will stop by."

"Are you okay?" Payton asked me.

I began to swing the crystal and watched as Payton's eyes obediently followed it left to right. I didn't understand the spell I was about to cast but knew I could access the Fae powers I needed.

"I was worried about you," Payton said.

My throat tightened. Maybe Payton would forget this had ever happened, but I wouldn't. I could never be her friend again if I wiped her memory.

"Payton, it's me," I whispered. Thankfully the shower was still on, I prayed Jaria was too busy to hear me speak. I stopped the crystal from swinging with my other hand.

The fog left her eyes.

I shielded the crystal from her view.

Payton looked at me. She shuddered as she met my gaze but didn't look away. "Alice?"

I nodded. "This is the real me."

"What are you?" she asked.

"I'm a Bigfoot."

"Who is that?" Payton glanced towards Jaria.

Tough question. "Jaria is my...supervisor," I replied.

Payton studied Jaria.

"Pretend you're getting hypnotized," I said.

She obeyed. I would never deserve her trust.

"I was given the gift of transformation and can appear human," It felt right to confess to Payton. "I was enrolled in the volleyball camp and then high school. I need to learn what it means to be human."

"What it means to be human?" Payton asked.

"My culture is different from yours."

"How?"

"I'll explain later," I said, "but this isn't the time. Jaria thinks I'm wiping your memory. Now that you know who I am, I don't want to take that from you. You're the best friend I've ever had, and I'm tired of keeping this a secret."

"Maybe it's safer to wipe my memory," Payton said.

"No." I needed her and had almost shouted. I prayed Jaria hadn't heard.

Payton studied me, hoping I'd explain.

"Pretending to be someone I'm not is hard," I said. "I need a friend, someone who knows."

Payton considered.

As I waited, I realized how selfish I was acting. I couldn't endanger Payton because I wanted one friend among the humans who knew what I was.

I began to swing the crystal.

"Don't do it," Payton murmured, eyes already glazing as she fell back under the spell.

"Really?" I asked.

She pulled her gaze away from the crystal and brought it to meet me. "You seriously can't tell me that my best friend is having the coolest adventure, and I'm not allowed to know?"

I laughed.

She smiled.

"We good?" I asked.

"We're good," she replied. "But you've got so much explaining to do once we're out of here."

I would've hugged her if it weren't for Jaria.

Instead, I lifted the pendant back over my head and allowed it to drop to my chest. I became human again.

"Does it hurt?" Payton asked.

I shook my head and pressed a finger to my lips.

Payton blanked her gaze.

I turned towards the mirror. By the miracle of transformation, my clothes were dry and unstained. My nose was bleeding, but the worst of it had stopped. I grabbed some paper towels and held them against my nose.

"It's done then?" Jaria said. I turned around but didn't see her. She was already invisible.

Lexi, Quinn, and Ellie seemed dazed.

Jaria snapped her fingers, and they sprung to life. I was glad to see Payton follow their example.

Lexi looked from the shower to my bloody nose. She shook her head and then walked from the locker room. Quinn and Ellie followed suit.

Payton turned towards me.

"I'll be a second," I told her, motioning to the bloody nose.

Dismissing her made me uncomfortable, but I thought Payton would understand.

I waited until I heard the door close.

"Why didn't you stop them?" I asked Jaria. A minute ago, I'd wanted to strangle her, but that was before my confession to Payton. That had stilled my anger.

Jaria didn't reply.

"That's the problem with you," I continued. "You're always keeping secrets from me. I didn't even know these crystals had any other powers! Now you asked me to brainwash my friend? How far were you going to let Lexi go before stepping in?"

"The job…" she said meekly. "You had to learn."

"To learn what?" I began shouting. "How to take a shower?"

"What it means to be human."

I pointed to the bloody shower and said, "That isn't what it means to be human."

"Maybe not a good person," she replied, "but human."

I tried to understand but failed. This whole time, I thought I couldn't get hurt. I thought I was impervious to danger with the humans because I had the Fae's protection.

But I was as vulnerable as the humans' fleshy skin.

I felt my eyes water, part of me wanted to cry. I couldn't understand how anyone could hate another person the way Lexi hated me…I couldn't grasp why Jaria would let me suffer.

I choked back the tears. I wasn't going to give Jaria the satisfaction of knowing how much this hurt me.

"It's okay," she said. The iciness from her voice was missing. I wanted to tell her how crushed I felt, but the truth was as real as my bloody nose: Jaria would never be my friend.

I turned off the shower and began to walk from the locker room.

"Alice?" Jaria said.

"Yes?" I turned back towards her voice.

"I've had news about your mother."

"What about Stepma?" I asked.

"Not her," Jaria hesitated. "Your real ma. Evie."

I refused to hope. "Ma's dead."

"She's not," Jaria said. "And this spring, we're going to find her."

I considered walking back to her. I wanted to ask questions, but Jaria was never free with information.

Then I thought of Payton, waiting for answers I could give.

"I can't wait to learn more," I said, walking from the locker room. "You can tell me later."

I went to the gym to find Payton. There were a lot of things that my friend deserved to be told.

Chapter 30

"Chicken?" Payton asked her mom after we unloaded the bus into the school parking lot.

"Rotisserie style," Tami replied, biting into a thigh piece. "Figured you girls might be hungry."

She was right, of course. Tami usually was when it came to food, but neither Payton or myself had expected a parking lot picnic. Tami had come prepared with chicken, grapes, bread, and plenty of napkins.

I pulled off a drumstick and began to eat. It was delicious, just like all the food Tami had shared with me.

Jaria had called to say she was running behind. I wasn't sure where she had gone after the fight in the locker room but had convinced myself that I didn't care.

"Sorry you lost," Tami said.

I shrugged. The pain of the lost game had long been replaced with fresh emotions. I was stunned Lexi had treated me the way she had and ecstatic that Payton finally knew my true identity.

"It's been a weird day," Payton said.

I nodded my agreement.

Payton had spent the afternoon asking me questions as we whispered at the top of the bleachers. She wanted to know everything about Bigfoot life, and I didn't hold anything back. After months of secrecy, I wanted to share everything with her.

Payton couldn't believe Jaria had watched when Lexi threw me in the shower. It was validating when Payton understood my abandonment, I was unsure if I had overreacted.

"Hey! Alice!"

I turned to see Mark stepping from the school. My heart fluttered at the sight of him.

I waved him over with a greasy hand. Then I set the chicken aside and desperately tried to wipe the oil from my fingers and face.

"This is my friend Mark, we have homeroom together," I said once he walked over. "This is my best friend and teammate Payton and her mom, Tami."

"Hungry?" Tami asked, already handing Mark a drumstick.

"No thanks, I'm a vegetarian," Mark said. "But I'll take some grapes?"

"When did you become a vegetarian?" I asked.

"Recent development," he said with a shrug. "Haven't told many people yet."

Tami laughed and asked after his family. She knew his parents and told him best of luck breaking the vegetarian news to them. Mark said he would take all the luck he could get.

"How did the game go?" Mark asked me.

"We lost," I replied. "But Payton and I had time to get to know each other better."

Payton and I made eye contact, and I grinned. The full nature of our conversation was our little secret.

"Sounds like a fine reason to skip school," Mark said.

I laughed. The others chuckled.

"Well, thanks for the fruit," Mark said. He turned towards me. "Alice, I'll see you in homeroom on Monday?"

"You sure will," I replied.

Mark walked away, and Payton studied me with her lips quirked in a half-grin.

"You have a crush on him!" Payton accused as soon as Mark was out of earshot.

Tami laughed so hard she had to cover her mouth to keep from losing her chicken.

"I do not!" I protested. "I have a boyfriend. Or suitor. Something." I didn't want to explain Dayton again in front of Tami. Bigfoot courtship rituals were so different from human ones.

Payton shrugged, considered, then said. "Well, you two do look kinda cute together."

"Do we?" I asked and immediately regretted speaking when Payton laughed. Maybe I did have a crush on Mark, but it wasn't anything I was going to act on. "But it doesn't matter. I can't see him right now."

"Maybe I'm selfish," Payton said, "but I'm hoping you have plenty of years left at Piner High School. You'll have your chance."

Chapter 31

"I hoped I'd find you here." The voice had come from behind me.

I turned around but already knew it was Daylen. The thought of him made me ache. I wanted his protection. Maybe if he held me tight enough, I'd feel safe again. Maybe, for a moment, I could pretend that I was a normal Bigfoot and Piner High School didn't exist.

My mood had shifted since the sunny parking lot picnic with Payton, Tami, and Mark. I finally had the chance to be alone for the first time all day and, for better or worse, I needed the time to think.

"I don't want to talk." I turned away from him. I had taken my necklace off and was turning the crystal in the light.

"Then you shouldn't be so predictable." He sat down beside me at the base of the tree. "I know where you like to hide."

"I'm hiding because I want to be left alone," I said with a growl.

He nodded. "Jaria thought I should talk to you."

"Jaria!" I laughed. "What would Jaria know about anything? One second she says she is looking out for me, and the next she says she can't help."

"Jaria seemed really worried about you," Daylen said.

"Did Jaria tell you what happened?"

"She only said I should talk to you. I thought you'd tell me what happened."

I had hoped he wouldn't ask about it. Daylen was always easy to talk to, and if he stayed with me long enough, I knew I'd tell him everything.

Only I didn't want to talk about it. Talking about it would be like reliving the humiliation again.

"I came here to be alone," I said.

"You can talk to me. I want to help," Daylen replied.

"If you want to help, leave me alone." I was beginning to shout and cry simultaneously. It wasn't a good look for me.

"Well, I'll just sit here next to you," he said. "Keep you company."

It was the last thing I needed. This was my spot, and he was the invader.

I looked up at the tree. I could climb. Daylen couldn't follow me. I was too big for the tree, but he was even larger than I was.

I dropped the pendant on the ground and jumped into the branches and began to move upwards.

The tree creaked under me as I climbed. Pa had warned me that the tree couldn't support me as an adult the way it had as a child. Right now, I didn't care.

"What are you doing?" Daylen shouted after me.

"Getting away from you!" I shouted back. I knew I must seem crazy to him, but I didn't want to talk.

I heard the scraping of branches below. Daylen was beginning to chase after me. I moved faster.

The tree creaked louder.

"Alice, this tree is old," he shouted up at me. "It's time to get down!"

Yet, I climbed. I knew I should stop, but I didn't want to. I could see everything from the top. I wouldn't have to face any of my real problems if I was hidden in the tree.

I pushed through my sobs and fought to reach a new height. Only a few more branches higher. Then Daylen wouldn't be able to reach me. Or see me. Or talk to me.

"Go away!" I yelled down to him.

"Fine," he said. I watched through the branches as he jumped from the tree back to the ground.

I heard a long creak.

There was a roar. The snapping of wood.

"Alice," Daylen yelled. "Get down! Now!"

Then gravity shifted.

My feet began to slip, and I grabbed the tree trunk, pulling my body against it with my arms.

The tree was falling, crashing.

I hugged the trunk with my legs as the branch slipped from under my feet. I was too high up to safely drop down to the earth.

I tried to keep my eyes open, but debris was beginning to fly everywhere.

After another long crash, my stomach dropped.

I was falling downward, clutching to the tree as it gave way to gravity and fell towards the earth. My arms ached, and my legs complained as I gripped the tree.

With a searing realization, I detected the direction of the fall. The tree was falling towards the boundary, and I was about to cross the magical perimeter.

The boundary should've been the least of my worries, I had crossed it endlessly in the last few months…

—except—

My pendant was back with Daylen. I couldn't transform. As soon as I crossed the boundary, I'd be exposed for the second time that day. The idea terrified me.

My arm slipped. The strain on all my other limbs increased.

My body was exhausted—strained from the volleyball match and Lexi's beating—but I held on. Despite my slipping limbs and rising panic, I needed to stay strong for another few seconds.

I tightened my legs around the tree and dared to lift my shifting arm long enough to resettle it.

I wouldn't fall. I told myself I wasn't going to fall off the tree.

Then, finally, the tree stopped moving. It bounced, settling into its new place.

I opened my eyes, relieved to see the ground a few feet below. I jumped down and noticed my dark fur. I was Bigfoot.

Then I checked the boundary. Somehow, it was still beyond me. It had extended several body-lengths beyond its usual position.

Just as the Fae had exposed me the day that I had discovered my powers, they could protect me now. This time, they chose to be there for me.

"Alice!" Daylen ran to me. He handed me the pendant and looked around. "The boundary's shifted."

Weakened, I fell to my knees. I worked to catch my breath. I picked the pendant from his hand and pulled it back over my neck. "The Fae have shifted it for me before."

He kneeled next to me, inspecting my arms where the branches had scraped my skin. "Doesn't look like anything serious."

"I think I'm okay," I said.

"Are you really?" he asked.

I inspected the pendant, debating if I really wanted to put it back on. "No, of course, I'm not okay."

Then, finally, to my embarrassment, I told him everything. My body was still throbbing with adrenaline, and I choked on tears as I spoke.

Regardless, Daylen listened.

I explained how I'd messed up Lexi's play. That Lexi had wanted to kick me when I was down, and she had taken my pendant away. I told him that I transformed in the locker room.

I confessed that I had tried to swipe Lexi. I told him how badly I had wanted to make her bleed.

I explained how Jaria had been there the whole time but didn't do anything until I was ready to hurt Lexi.

Finally, I confessed that I didn't wipe Payton's memory.

He laughed at that. "Jaria's going to be furious when she finds out about Payton."

I laughed, gulping for breath through the tears. "Yes, Jaria is going to be so mad! But it's worth it."

"I'm glad you have Payton too," Daylen said. There was a hardness in his tone. If I accepted Payton in my life, it meant he couldn't be my suitor.

He waited in silence until my tears subsided. Then Daylen stood, shaking the dirt from his fur. He helped me stand beside him.

We began walking to the village side by side.

When we reached the tree stump, I turned towards it. My tree was dead. Roots spreading from a splintered stump. I'd seen fallen trees before, but this was like the body of a friend. I thought the tears would come again.

But I was done crying. Instead, I finally knew what needed to be done.

"Is everything okay?" Daylen asked.

"Daylen," I began, speaking slow. I didn't want to say what I needed to tell him.

"What is it?" He turned to me. He still held my hand in his.

My eyes met his hazel ones. I had found my clarity.

I wanted him to become my mate, but there was something bigger that I wanted to do more. If I had been anybody else, I would have chosen him.

"I can't be your mate," I said.

"What?" He was surprised. Then again, so was I, but it was suddenly apparent what I needed to do.

"I've been given a power I don't understand," I said. "But it was always meant for me."

I'd been given a fantastic gift: the ability to see the world from a different perspective. I knew that human technology far exceeded our own and that the Fae could only hide us for so much longer. My people needed someone to learn human ways.

"I don't fully understand everything," I squeezed his hand. Even now, I sought his comfort. "But I can't give this up."

"So, you'll give me up instead?" he asked.

The question hurt. I tried to find the courage to meet his gaze again but looked down instead.

"We both knew it was going to end this way," I said. It was true, but it had been easier for both of us while we had pretended otherwise.

It took him a moment to reply.

Finally, he cleared his throat and asked, "Was it good? While we lasted, were we good?"

Finally, I met his gaze.

"You've been an amazing suitor," I said. "If things were different, I might have become your mate."

"Really?" he asked.

I nodded and held back tears so I could say one final thing. "This has been so wonderful that I'm worried I'll regret this. Thank you for everything."

I stood on my toes to kiss his cheek. Then I released his hand, turned away, and walked to my home.

I was sweaty and bloody. My heart was broken and betrayed. My mind raced on fumes. Now that I had made my choice, there was so much work that needed to be done.

But first, I needed a bath in the river.

Epilogue

The bonfire burned hot on the Winter Solstice.

I stood near the front, shadowing Mother Gazina and Jaria. For all appearances, I was another apprentice. The exact nature of my training was kept private. Only my family knew. And Daylen.

Daylen stood with the other adolescents, Nila by his side. She'd be his suitor this season. I wished I could hate her with the same ferocity that I missed Daylen. But I didn't. Nila was a good, sweet female. If I couldn't be Daylen's mate, she'd make an excellent alternative. I was happy for them, and it was making me miserable.

Pa and Stepma had invited me to stand with them tonight since I didn't have a suitor. But I couldn't. I wasn't a child any longer. I couldn't stand with them any better than I could with the other adolescents.

Instead, my place was with Mother Gazina and Jaria. Esteemed and outcast at the same time. Different.

Mother Gazina finished the Ceremony. Tonight should've been my opportunity to reestablish friendships with the other adolescents. However, since Daylen and I ended our suitorship, being with the others my age wasn't fun. I couldn't talk about my life with them any better than I could tell the humans I was a Bigfoot.

Except for Payton. I finally had one human friend who knew.

It didn't take long before Jaria learned I hadn't wiped Payton's memory, but by the time Jaria knew it was too late. The Fae couldn't safely modify Payton's memory and allowed my transgression. Jaria was still angry with me, but having Payton's awareness was worth Jaria's anger.

I watched Daylen and Nila walk to the community house together. I fought the urge to follow Daylen and tell him that I'd passed my first semester of human high school. I wanted to brag that my grades had even been solid. But that didn't seem like a good idea.

Daylen and I had tried trapping together after the tree fell, but it'd been too strange. We could be friendly acquaintances, but I'd lost him as a companion.

I turned from the village and began walking through the snow-covered trees. Bryson tried to follow me, but I told him I wanted to be alone. He said he was worried about me, but he let me go.

I walked without thinking, my feet taking me to my fallen tree. I sat near the stump and waited for the pain to pass. I'd be waiting for a long time.

I smelled him before I saw him, before I heard him.

Human.

I looked into the forest, right beyond the boundary. The moon was bright, but I waited until I saw his movement to be sure.

It was Mark. He wasn't carrying his bow, he had an instrument instead.

He found a log, brushed off the snow, and sat down. He began to play a song, it sounded like something I'd heard from the radio.

I listened, but the boundary garbled the sound.

Mark began to sing, and I only had a sense of his voice. I needed more.

So, I crossed the boundary to hear him better.

up next
A Bigfoot's Quest

Alice's dual identities as Bigfoot and human are starting to feel natural. Spring break arrives, and Alice is ready for some needed much-needed rest.

But when Jaria reveals the location of Alice's ma, they embark on a new adventure—one that yields more questions than answers. And it isn't long before Alice is seeking something different: the truth.

Meanwhile, Alice must question her relationship with Mark; can he care for her as she really is? Spring break is looking pretty crazy, so thank goodness she has Payton—assuming Alice can keep her best-friend from following her into trouble.

Follow Alice's adventures in the sequel: *A Bigfoot's Quest.* Coming late-spring 2020.

Author's Note

A lot of things had to fall apart before this book could be written. I wish I could say "it all fell together for the best," but that's not me. Instead, I'll say: I'm glad to have made it here, there was a time I wasn't sure I would.

This book wasn't created in isolation. Huge shout out to those who contributed to this project: Josh for believing in me enough to help shape this opportunity, Geneva for her constant support and volleyball discussions, Suzanne for on-point editing, and Alicia for discussions on indie publishing and reminding me that perfection is the enemy of done.

I hope you've enjoyed Alice's adventure and happy reading!

Mel Braxton

About the Author

Mel Braxton is based in Portland, OR, where she daydreams of sasquatch, mermaids, and aliens. She likes to make cute noises, sing made-up songs, and slide on hardwood while wearing socks. If you've liked this book and want to read more, check out the following:

Website: [melbraxton.com]
Facebook: [@MeleneBraxton]
Instagram: [@MeleneBraxton]
Newsletter: [http://bit.ly/melbraxton]

Also By Mel Braxton

The Wild Mermaid (releasing April 1, 2020)
Cora was thrilled to reach the gates of Atlantis. Now appointed as the Queen's soloist, she discovers her mermaid migration was a trick and begins her escape a seaweed-bed of lies. It's a journey that'll ultimately transform her into *The Wild Mermaid.*

Illiam
A sentient planet called Illiam had been alone for eons, and when Elysa crash-lands on its surface, the two begin an unlikely relationship. (A novella)

Living Without the Dead
A poetic memoir that explores a parent's battle and eventual death to cancer. (published as Myra Bates)